P9-CCZ-230

A

KILLER ANGELS

COMPANION

BY D. SCOTT HARTWIG

THOMAS PUBLICATIONS
Gettysburg PA 17325

Copyright © 1996 by D. Scott Hartwig

Printed and bound in the United States of America

Published by THOMAS PUBLICATIONS
             P.O. Box 3031
             Gettysburg, Pa. 17325

All rights reserved. No part of this book may be used or reproduced without written permission of the author and the publisher, except in the case of brief quotations embodied in critical essays and reviews.

ISBN-0-939631-95-4

Cover design by Ryan C. Stouch

The maps on pages 2 and 18 were executed by Thomas A. Desjardin.

Photo Credits

Gettysburg National Military Park — 19
Library of Congress — 25
Maine State Archives — 20 & 21
National Archives — 30
Thomas Publications — 27 (top)
U.S. Army Military History Institute — 9, 12, 15, 17, 27 (bottom), 33, 35, 37, 39, 41, 43 & 45

Cover photo courtesy of Dean S. Thomas and the Gettysburg National Military Park. This is a portion of the "New York" Gettysburg Cyclorama.

CONTENTS

INTRODUCTION
&
ACKNOWLEDGEMENTS

At least ten years ago a cousin of mine, Jim Stehli, who was attending high school in Japan as a Rotary exchange student had a script translated from English to Japanese for an orientation program we offered at Gettysburg National Military Park. As a thank you we sent him several items. One was the novel *The Killer Angels*. Several years ago I was speaking with his mother about this book when she told me that on an application for an MBA program he had listed the book as one of his favorite works of fiction. The odd thing was that my cousin had little interest in the American Civil War. It may have been the only Civil War book he read in quite a while. I realized then how powerful and moving Michael Shaara's work was. If it could reach out to a well read, highly intelligent high school student in Japan, Shaara had connected.

I am a historian. Consequently, I originally looked down upon Shaara's work. After all, it was fiction. But the fact that my cousin, who I respected, as well as other people I knew, had such a high opinion of the book, I decided to read it again. This time I discarded my prejudice as a historian—or tried very hard to—and found that there was more to this novel than met the eye. It held deeper meaning than simply to tell the story of the Battle of Gettysburg, and it was beautifully written. I gained a greater respect for this fine piece of literature. Still, the number of people who read this novel and came away thinking they had read a history of the battle, annoyed me. Then Dean Thomas suggested I write a primer for people who had read the novel to analyze just how Shaara's version of the Battle of Gettysburg stacked up against a historian's reconstruction of those same events. This is the result of that suggestion.

Others must share the credit for this work: Dean Thomas, for conceiving the idea, and Sally Rodgers, my editor, who made this a better book. And, my wife, Cindi, who patiently tolerated the many hours I spent writing.

THE KILLER ANGELS—
THE NOVEL AS HISTORY

It is a good bet that more people will read Michael Shaara's Pulitzer Prize winning novel *The Killer Angels* than any other book on the Battle of Gettysburg. Shaara's book is immensely successful not only because he writes well, but also because he presents the battle as a compelling human drama. Even those who would never dare to pick up a history book find it impossible to put his book down. *The Killer Angels* does not focus upon strategy and tactics, or the chess-like movements of units upon the battlefield. Instead, *The Killer Angels* is about people—soldiers—who are caught up in a terrible and desperate battle. Through these men the reader experiences the grim and gritty reality of command in battle. The characters—with one major exception—are not fictitious creations of Shaara's pen, but are historical personalities of the battle. For the Confederates, Shaara selects Lee, Longstreet, Pickett, and Armistead. Buford, Hancock, and Chamberlain are the principal Federals. All of them are officers whose stories or relationship to the battle fascinated Shaara. Through each of these men and their personal struggles he tells the story of the battle, exposing the harsh truth of command and the anguishing decisions these leaders must make that will send other men, or themselves, to injury or death. It is this human touch that readers can identify with and understand, and which makes *The Killer Angels* so appealing to such a diverse group of readers.

Shaara makes the claim in his foreword that he turned to primary sources to write the book. "I have not consciously changed any fact," he writes. Shaara's story is told so well, his character portrayals are so believable, that the unknowing reader might believe what they are reading *is* history. It is important, then, to examine the novel against what the soldiers who fought the Battle of Gettysburg and historians who have studied the engagement carefully have recorded. How faithful to history is *The Killer Angels*? If Shaara took liberty and license with his characters and their actions, where and why did he do so? And, if he did, what really happened? These are some of the questions to be explored. This is not to denigrate this magnificent novel in any way. It is a classic work of Civil War fiction and justly deserves the laurels it has garnered.

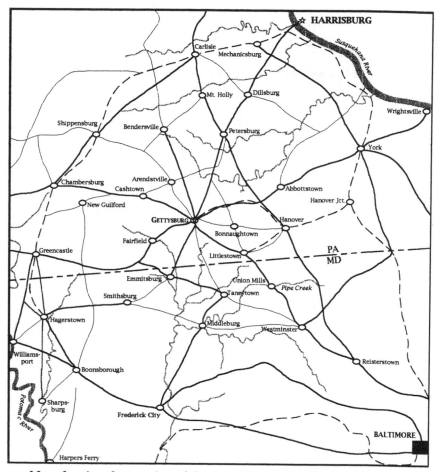

Map showing that portion of the area of operations in the Gettysburg campaign between Baltimore, Md. and Harrisburg, Pa.

❖ ❖ ❖

James Longstreet emerges as a favorite of Shaara in the pages of *The Killer Angels*. In the foreword, where Shaara introduces the characters of the book, he describes Longstreet as one of the new soldiers who has sensed the change that improved weaponry had wrought upon tactics. Shaara writes, "he has invented a trench and a new theory of defensive warfare." Longstreet was a thoroughly competent soldier but few would have deemed him inventive or one of the "new soldiers." The trench had been employed in warfare since the days of the Romans; its benefits were well known by the time of the American Civil War. If anyone in the Army of Northern Virginia understood the value

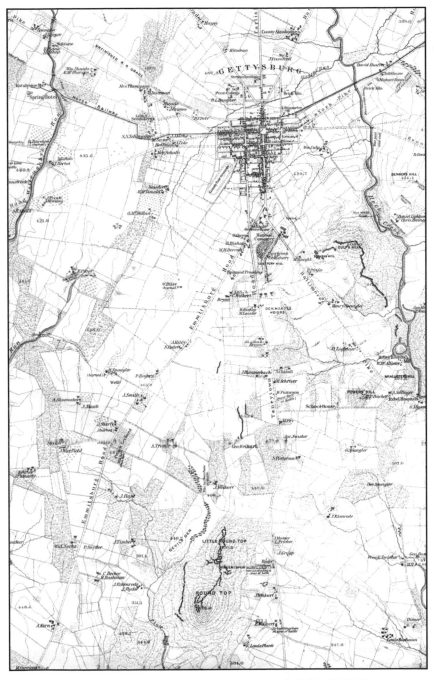

The Warren map of the Gettysburg Battlefield, 1868/69.

of trenches and fortifications it was Robert E. Lee. When Lee assumed command of the Army of Northern Virginia in June 1862, he set his troops to digging extensive fortifications around Richmond, which earned him the short-lived nickname "The King of Spades." But Lee also understood the South could not fight a war behind fortifications and trenches and hope to win.

It is equally debatable that Longstreet was ahead of his time in tactical theory. He offered no imaginative or dramatic changes in tactics at any time during the war. After the crushing Confederate victory at Fredericksburg, however, he became an advocate for the tactical defensive. There, Confederate riflemen behind stone walls and earthworks had mowed down Union soldiers attacking over open ground. But the Confederates were able to employ these defensive tactics with success at Fredericksburg because the Union commander, Ambrose Burnside, obliged them by attacking Lee precisely where he wanted him to. Had Lee attempted to repeat these same tactics in May, 1863, against Joseph Hooker, whose army numbered 130,000 to Lee's 60,000, he very likely would have suffered a defeat. But he assumed the offensive, stole the initiative from Hooker, and defeated the Federal army. Lee understood that the key to successful generalship was to use whatever tactics offered the best hope of success, depending upon the circumstances, and the personality of the opponent. There was no pat formula for victory in the Civil War.

During the late afternoon of July 1, Lee and Longstreet debate the tactics to be employed at Gettysburg. Shaara's sympathy is clearly with Longstreet in the conflict the 1st Corps commander has with Lee over the manner in which the battle is to be fought. Lee presents his plan to renew the battle against the Federal army at Gettysburg, while Longstreet advocates a sweeping turning movement to the south to get between the Union army and Washington, D. C. Longstreet's plan sounds sensible, but Shaara's Lee has his blood up and dismisses Longstreet's suggestion, unable to see its merit in his desire to crush the enemy in his front. Reality differed sharply from this version. Before settling upon a plan for July 2, Lee weighed and considered every option open to him—including Longstreet's suggestion for a strategic turning movement. The problem with Longstreet's plan was that Lee knew very little about the whereabouts of most of the Union army. He had two of the seven Union army corps in his front on July 1. The position of the other five was unknown, except that they were somewhere south of Gettysburg. Had Lee adopted Longstreet's strategy, without "Jeb" Stuart's absent cavalry to screen and scout such a maneuver, he risked stumbling into the enemy on unfamiliar ground— precisely what had occurred on July 1. Luck had been with the army that day and they had defeated the Federals. The next time the Union army might be better prepared and in greater numbers. Lee settled upon his plan to fight the Army of the Potomac at Gettysburg, not because he had lost his composure in his excitement to get at the enemy, or because he was too exhausted to consider another option, but because he believed it offered the best prospect for success to his army under the less than ideal conditions he faced.[1]

In Chapter 3 the reader encounters Union cavalry General John Buford. Shaara's Buford is a tough, cynical old regular who is disgusted with the incompetent Union generalship he has endured, but continues to perform because he is a professional. He is a loner who does not even know the name of some of the officers on his staff, having learned long ago not to get too close to anyone or learn their names unless absolutely necessary. The real John Buford possessed some of the characteristics of Shaara's Buford. He was tough, and sickened by the incompetence he had seen exhibited in the war. A member of Meade's staff wrote that Buford, "is of a good natured disposition but not to be trifled with." Another soldier related that Buford, "despised the false flourish and noisy parade of the charlatans of his service," and that his bravery, coolness, and the care he took of his soldiers, "endeared him to all." In contrast to Shaara's Buford, the real soldier knew every man on his staff very well and took a personal interest in their lives and families. His closeness to his men is reflected by the fact that he would die in the arms of one of his faithful staff officers, Captain Myles Keough, of Little Big Horn fame.[2]

Buford was an innovative soldier. He advocated equipping troopers with breech-loading weapons and he trained his men in the tactics of fighting dismounted. But he had not "thrown away the silly sabers and the damned dragoon pistols." Neither had he provided his cavalry with repeating weapons. His cavalry at Gettysburg were armed with breech-loading, single shot carbines. As for the sabers and dragoon pistols, there was nothing silly about them in close combat. Sabers never ran out of ammunition, and the pistol was superior to the carbine in close-in cavalry fighting. At the big cavalry battle at Brandy Station on June 9, 1863, Buford's troopers used both of these weapons to good advantage against Confederate cavalry. The variety of weapons gave a cavalryman versatility, and allowed him to engage enemy infantry or cavalry.[3]

Buford arrived in Gettysburg on June 30, 1863, not to a deserted town, but one whose citizens flocked out to the streets to cheer his regiments as they rode through town. Confederates under General Jubal Early had passed through the borough on June 26 frightening everyone, so the arrival of Union soldiers was a welcome sight. Lieutenant John H. Calef, commanding the artillery of Buford's Division, recalled:

> Such was the joy of the people at the appearance of Buford and his veterans that the city presented a gala-day appearance. The school children, dressed in white and carrying bouquets and wreaths of flowers, were assembled on the corners of the streets singing patriotic songs.[4]

Buford led his division to the ridges west of Gettysburg. Here, in Shaara's version, Buford studies the ground and concludes this is the only place to give battle; there is no good ground south of Gettysburg. He fears that the Confederates will seize the high ground immediately south of the town (Culp's Hill, Cemetery Hill, Cemetery Ridge) and dig in, forcing the Union army to attack. The attack, he is certain, will end in disaster.[5]

The problem with this version is its presumption that Gettysburg was the only place to fight a battle in all of south-central Pennsylvania and northern Maryland. Buford knew this was not true. There were many places south of Gettysburg that qualified as "good ground" by Civil War terms. Meade hoped to fight against Lee at one of those points, behind Little Pipe Creek near Taneytown, Maryland. The terrain offered decided advantages to its defender, but this position would have been "good ground" only if Lee attacked Meade there. If he had outmaneuvered Meade and forced a battle elsewhere, the ground at Pipe Creek would have been irrelevant. The high ground at Gettysburg only mattered if the two armies clashed in its vicinity. Had Lee seized the high ground at Gettysburg on July 1 as Shaara's Buford fears, it is unlikely that Meade would have attacked him. Meade had prepared a contingency plan to assemble the army behind Pipe Creek. Had Lee captured the key terrain at Gettysburg in the first day of fighting, Meade almost certainly would have drawn his army back to this point.

The real Buford sensed when he arrived at Gettysburg that if Meade decided to offer Lee battle there, the Union army would need to hold the high ground south of town. Therefore, he made plans to defend the approaches to Gettysburg, not because it was the only "good ground," but because as a good cavalry officer it was his duty to anticipate the possibility that his army might make its battle there and act accordingly.

One of Buford's greatest strengths as a cavalry officer was his ability to gather information, accurately assess it, and relay the pertinent facts to his superiors. In the novel Buford sends a message to Major General John F. Reynolds, the 1st Corps commander, which reads: "Have occupied Gettysburg. Contacted large party of Reb infantry. I think they are coming this way. Expect they will be here in force in the morning."[6] The real Buford would have considered this unacceptably shoddy intelligence work. Compare it with the dispatch that Buford really sent to Reynolds:

> I am satisfied that A. P. Hill's corps is massed just back of Cashtown, about 9 miles from this place. Pender's division of this (Hill's) corps came up to-day—of which I advised you, saying "The enemy in my front is increased." The enemy's pickets (infantry and artillery) are within 4 miles of this place, on the Cashtown road. My parties have returned that went north, northwest, and northeast, after crossing the road from Cashtown to Oxford in several places. They

6

heard nothing of any force having passed over it lately. The road, however, is terribly infested with prowling cavalry parties. Near Heidlersburg to-day, one of my parties captured a courier of Lee's. Nothing was found on him. He says Ewell's corps is crossing the mountains from Carlisle, Rodes' division being at Petersburg in advance. Longstreet, from all I can learn, is still behind Hill. I have many rumors and reports of the enemy advancing upon mc from toward York. I have to pay attention to some of them, which causes me to overwork my horses and men.[7]

The difference between the two messages is manifest to even the most non-military mind. The first one provides only the vaguest information and only one fact—that Buford has occupied Gettysburg. This message would have been of little value to Reynolds. The real message, by contrast, is full of facts and specific information that help Reynolds form a picture of the Confederate army's dispositions.

Early on the morning of July 1, Buford's Division was attacked by Confederate infantry of Heth's Division. In the novel Buford's troopers are dug in and forced to repulse repeated attacks by waves of Heth's infantry. The fighting is furious and, at times, hand-to-hand. It makes for thrilling reading but the real engagement was not nearly as dramatic or bloody.

The role of Buford's cavalry was not to engage enemy infantry in a stand-up fight, but to harass and attempt to delay them. Despite Shaara's repeated references to the cavalry being "dug in," no one was dug in. Cavalry units were light, mobile forces that did not even carry entrenching tools. Although much is made of Buford's breech-loading carbines, they possessed an effective range of only about 100 yards. Heth's infantryman were armed with muzzle-loading rifles that had a range of nearly 300 yards. Buford's troopers could shoot faster, but Heth's infantry had them completely outranged. Also, to fight effectively against infantry, cavalry had to dismount. One of every four troopers was detailed to hold the horses, which reduced the strength on the firing line by one-quarter. In a stand-up fight against infantry, cavalry could not hope to stand long.

Buford's tactics on July 1 were to harass Heth and force him to deploy his division, not engage him in a pitched battle such as Shaara describes. For Heth to deploy his division of 7,000 soldiers from column (which moved faster) to line (which was the fighting formation) was a time consuming movement, and time was the prize Buford sought. He dismounted the main body of Gamble's Brigade to fight on foot and engage the Confederate advance. When the pressure became too great the troopers withdrew to their horses, which provided them the mobility to maneuver to a new defensive position rapidly. The ensuing engagement between Buford's dismounted troopers and Heth's infantry amounted to little more than skirmishing—not the fierce conflict of the novel. Colonel Birkett Fry, the colonel of the 13th Alabama Infantry, Heth's Division, who directly confronted Gamble's dismounted troopers wrote of the engagement:

> With reference to the resistance made by the Union cavalry to the advance of Archer's Brigade in the morning of July 1st my recollection is clear that it was inconsiderate. I conversed yesterday on the subject with one of my Captains (James W. Simpson) who was present. He agrees with me that up to the time we encountered the Infantry, our advance was not retarded and that the cavalry did us no damage.[8]

Fry's statement is supported by the number of casualties suffered by Buford's cavalry on July 1. He lost 127 killed, wounded and captured, approximately 4 percent of his effective strength. Not all of these casualties were suffered in the fight with Heth; some occurred during the fighting of the late afternoon. An infantryman would have considered the skirmishing performed by Buford's cavalry to be relatively safe compared to the lethal encounter of infantry versus infantry. Compare the losses of Buford's entire division of some 3,000 troopers with the casualties suffered by a single Union infantry regiment of 302 officers and men, the 2nd Wisconsin Infantry, which relieved Buford's troopers. In one volley from Archer's Brigade of Heth's Division, the 2nd had 116 officers and men shot down out of 302 effectives. Such disparity in losses gave rise to the often expressed contemptuous remark by infantry to passing cavalry: "Who ever saw a dead cavalryman." But because Buford's cavalry did not suffer great losses, it does not diminish the importance of what they accomplished on July 1.[9]

❖ ❖ ❖

One of the more controversial aspects of the Battle of Gettysburg was the Confederate failure to capture Cemetery Hill and Culp's Hill on the evening of July 1. Shaara leaves no doubt as to who was responsible: Confederate 2nd Corps commander Lt. General Richard S. Ewell. He depicts Ewell as indecisive, overly cautious, and generally unfit for the position he occupies. General Isaac Trimble is so incensed at his caution on July 1 that he labels him "a disgrace" to Lee, and refuses to serve under him any longer. At one point Ewell even admits to Lee that he had been too careful and too slow.[10]

Ever since the Confederate defeat at Gettysburg, Ewell has been a favorite scapegoat of Confederate veterans and historians. Shaara's portrayal of Ewell is not original. During the postwar era, a number of former Confederate officers, including Isaac Trimble, seeking to assign responsibility for the Confederate defeat at Gettysburg, assailed Ewell's performance there, particularly his failure to capture Cemetery Hill on July 1. General John B. Gordon, a brigade commander in Ewell's 2nd Corps, wrote in his memoirs that in "less than half

Lt. Gen. Richard S. Ewell   *Maj. Gen. Isaac R. Trimble*

an hour my troops would have swept up and over those hills," had Ewell permitted it. Others could not resist the temptation to compare Ewell unfavorably with his former commander, Stonewall Jackson, pointing out that had Ewell shown the spirit of Jackson, he would have taken Cemetery Hill. Douglas S. Freeman, the most influential historian of the Army of Northern Virginia, in his distinguished study, *Lee's Lieutenants*, titled one of his chapters on Gettysburg, "Ewell Cannot Reach a Decision." Its content, as might be surmised from the title, does not portray Ewell in a favorable light. Confronted with such damning evidence, it is not surprising that Shaara depicts Ewell so pathetically.[11] There is little disagreement among historians that Ewell does not belong in the company of great soldiers. He possessed positive limitations as a soldier at corps command. However, his critics—employing the benefit of hindsight—have judged his actions on July 1 unfairly. He performed far better under difficult circumstances than has generally been acknowledged.

On the morning of July 1 when Ewell learned that A. P. Hill had encountered Union forces west of Gettysburg, he promptly started Rodes' and Early's Divisions marching to Hill's assistance. He informed General Lee of this decision and received a message in reply which stated that if Ewell found the enemy force "very large" Lee wished to avoid a general engagement until the rest of the army was up. When Ewell arrived on the northern edge of the battlefield he realized that avoiding an engagement was impossible and he pressed the battle aggressively against the Federals. During the next three and one-half hours of fighting his corps decisively defeated the Union troops in his front and swept them from the field, scooping up over 3,000 prisoners in the victory. Despite cautionary orders from Lee, Ewell had pressed the battle with a combativeness that would have pleased even Jackson; he had been far from indecisive up to this point.

When Ewell entered Gettysburg he concluded to attack Cemetery Hill, if A. P. Hill would support the attack with his corps. About this time Ewell received a report from one of his brigade commanders of a large Union force approaching the battlefield from the east, along the York Pike. Unable to ignore the report, he dispatched two brigades to investigate. The report proved to be false, but it cost precious time. Meanwhile, Ewell learned that he could expect no help from Hill's Corps, which meant that if he assaulted Cemetery Hill, his men would do so unsupported, against the most formidable point of the hill. Then came an order from Lee directing Ewell to capture Cemetery Hill "if practicable." Ewell's critics claimed that he could have taken this hill easily had he made the effort. Just how easily is debatable. Union Major General Winfield S. Hancock, who was helping to rally and organize the defeated Union troops on Cemetery Hill, sent a dispatch to General Meade at 5:10 p.m. which stated that "this hill cannot well be taken," a strong statement from a tough Union officer that deserves attention. General Robert Rodes, commanding one of Ewell's divisions, reported that "the enemy had begun to establish a line of battle on the heights back of the town, and by the time my line was in a condition to renew the attack, he displayed quite a formidable line of infantry and artillery immediately in my front." Clearly it would not have been a simple task to capture Cemetery Hill. A well coordinated attack strongly supported by artillery would have been necessary, and even then there were no guarantees that the hill could have been taken.[12]

Ewell concluded not to attempt an assault upon Cemetery Hill. For this reason, he has been labeled as indecisive. But he had made a decision—that storming the hill without Hill's support was not practicable. Was it the right decision? Armed with the advantage of hindsight, it probably was not; an effort at least should have been attempted. But Ewell had no such advantage. He operated under circumstances that were highly uncertain—the whereabouts of most of the Union army was still unknown—and fraught with danger and tension. Dr. Gary Gallagher, in *The First Day at Gettysburg*, notes that Lee must bear some responsibility for the failure to capture Cemetery Hill on July 1. He writes: "Anyone seeking to apportion responsibility for what transpired on the Confederate side on the opening day at Gettysburg should look first to the commanding general."[13]

Rivaling the controversy generated by Ewell's failure to seize Cemetery Hill on July 1 is Lee's battle plan for July 2 and the pivotal role James Longstreet played in it. Shaara describes Lee as narrow-mindedly obsessed with the offensive—or perhaps with judgement impaired by his "illness." Whichever, Lee looks like a general well off his form. His orders are for Longstreet to attack up the Emmitsburg Road with McLaws' and Hood's Divisions. The attack is to be *en echelon*—an attack formation that resembles waves striking a beach. Longstreet is not pleased with the plan of attack, but he voices no objections and marches off like a good soldier to do Lee's bidding. When his command arrives at the front and finds the situation changed, and Hood pleads for permission to outflank the Union line, Longstreet must refuse him permission. He will obey Lee's orders, even though he knows those orders will cause the death and wounds of hundreds of his men, because it is what Lee expects and because Longstreet cannot go against Lee. The real battle—and what the veterans had to say about it, and about James Longstreet's behavior—differed dramatically from Shaara's recounting.

Lee's plan for July 2 was not to attack the Union position frontally, but to execute a turning movement with Longstreet's Corps that would strike the left flank of the Union army. Early on the morning of the 2nd he had ordered Captain Samuel R. Johnston, an engineer officer on his HQ staff, Major J. J. Clarke, of Longstreet's engineers, and two or three other men, to reconnoiter the enemy's left and attempt to locate their flank. According to Johnston, the party reached the summit of Little Round Top, which they found unoccupied. Johnston did not see the Union 3rd Corps, which had massed on low ground to the north but was masked from his view by woods. From Johnston's observations, the Union left rested upon Cemetery Ridge, a good one-half mile north of Little Round Top. Johnston and his party returned to Lee probably around 9 a.m. and reported their findings. Their report confirmed Lee's belief that the Union left flank was vulnerable to attack.[14]

Lee questioned Captain Johnston closely about how far he had gone on his reconnaissance. The Round Tops were a particular concern and Johnston assured him that he had found them unoccupied. Based upon Johnston's report Lee believed he could outflank the Federal position by moving Longstreet to the right and having him guide his attack north along the Emmitsburg Road so as to strike the reported flank of the enemy.

Meanwhile, Longstreet's two divisions (minus Evander Law's Brigade, which was marching hard to reach the front) had arrived on the edge of the first day's battlefield at approximately 8 or 8:30 a.m. and stacked arms to await their orders. Lee sent for Major General Lafayette McLaws, who Shaara describes as "a patient man, stubborn and slow, not brilliant, but a dependable soldier." In reality, of his three division commanders, McLaws, Hood, and Pickett, Longstreet considered McLaws the best soldier. When McLaws arrived at Lee's headquarters, Lee showed him a map and explained that he wanted McLaws to take his division to a point perpendicular to the Emmitsburg Road—

evidently in the area of the Peach Orchard. He asked McLaws if he thought he could reach the point indicated undetected. McLaws thought it possible but, unfamiliar with the ground, asked permission to reconnoiter the route. Lee agreed and offered to send Captain Johnston along to orient McLaws. Longstreet, who had been pacing back and forth behind the two men, interrupted and refused to permit McLaws to leave his division. Pointing to a map, he said he wanted McLaws to place his division at right angles to the position Lee had indicated. Lee calmly corrected Longstreet. At this point McLaws again requested permission to scout the route of march and again Longstreet refused. McLaws recalled: "General Longstreet appeared as if he was irritated and annoyed, but the cause I did not ask." He left the two generals and returned to his division.[15]

In the novel Longstreet thinks Lee's plan just might work, although the losses will be heavy. However, he requests permission from Lee to delay his movement until the Alabama brigade of Brigadier General Evander Law arrives. Law's Brigade, of Hood's Division, had been guarding trains near Chambersburg, some twenty-four miles away. They had been relieved and marched at 3 a.m. on July 2 to rejoin their division.[16]

The real Longstreet was not so agreeable to Lee's plan. The actual events that transpired after the meeting between Lee, McLaws, and Longstreet contrasted sharply with Shaara's version. The discussion between these men ended

Maj. Gen. Lafayette McLaws

12

around 9 a.m. Whether Lee had given Longstreet direct orders to commence his movement is not firmly established. However, the evidence strongly suggests that Lee had clearly made his plans known to Longstreet and expected them to be carried out without the need for a direct order. This was consistent with the manner in which Lee conducted business. He explained his plans and intentions to his subordinates, then expected that they would demonstrate the necessary initiative to see that they were carried out. Lee departed after his meeting with Longstreet and McLaws to visit Ewell and his left flank. He returned around 10 a.m. and, according to his military secretary Colonel A. L. Long, displayed impatience that Longstreet had not commenced his movement.[17]

What had Longstreet done during Lee's visit with Ewell? Apparently, he had done nothing. It is likely that he delayed his movement to wait for Law's Brigade and Pickett's Division. In contrast to the novel, he had not requested permission from Lee to delay his march until these troops arrived. Irritated by the delay in the day's operations, Lee now gave Longstreet a direct order to commence his movement. Longstreet requested permission to delay his march until Law arrived. He was willing to move without Pickett, but only reluctantly. He remarked to Hood that he did not like to go into action with only two of his three divisions.[18]

Law's Brigade arrived around noon and Longstreet immediately started his march. This march was not one of the most distinguished movements in the history of the Army of Northern Virginia. Edwin Coddington, one of the most careful historians of the battle, called it, "a comedy of errors such as one might expect of inexperienced commanders and raw militia, but not of Lee's 'war horse' and veteran troops." In the novel Lee assigns Captain Johnston, the engineer who performed the morning reconnaissance, to conduct Longstreet's Corps into its attack position. But Captain Johnston admits to Longstreet that he is unfamiliar with the roads Longstreet will use. Of course the real culprit is Major General J. E. B. Stuart, who is responsible for screening the army's movements and whose absence has created this unpleasant situation. Longstreet accepts this problem stoically and orders Captain Johnston to do the best he can and lead on.[19]

Although it is convenient to blame Stuart for Longstreet's troubled march, the problems that plagued it could have been avoided had Longstreet not shirked his responsibility. The movement of his two divisions to the right of the army was his responsibility alone. Captain Johnston, contrary to Shaara's version, had no orders from Lee to guide the 1st Corps march. "I was ordered by General Lee to 'ride with Gen'l Longstreet,' that is all the instructions I received," wrote Johnston in 1878. Longstreet saw things differently. He recalled in his memoirs: "General Lee ordered his reconnoitering officer to lead the troops of the First Corps and conduct them by a route concealed from view

13

of the enemy. As I was relieved for the time from the march, I rode near the middle of the line." During the postwar era Captain Johnston caught wind of Longstreet's attempt to shift the responsibility of the 1st Corps' poorly conducted march to his shoulders. He responded in a private letter:

> I had no idea where he (Longstreet) was going, except what I did infer from the movement having been ordered soon after I made my report...General Longstreet says that he rode at the rear of the column and conducted the movement of McLaws Division. Gen'l Longstreet is certainly mistaken. I am sure I rode with him during the entire march....

Even more damning was Johnston's observation in a letter to Lafayette McLaws in 1892. "Longstreet did not move off very promptly, nor was our march at all rapid. It did not strike me that General Longstreet was in a hurry to get into position. It might have been thought hurrying was unnecessary." What makes Johnston's correspondence on this issue so significant was his desire to keep his views private. He had no grudge against Longstreet, nor any wish to do him damage. He merely wanted the truth to be told.[20]

The 1st Corps march continued without incident until it arrived at a high point near the Hagerstown Road, which would expose the troops to a Union signal station that had been established on Little Round Top. Before the column reached that point Johnston advised Longstreet that continuing in the direction they were then marching would expose them to the enemy signalmen. In the novel, this same incident occurs but the implication is that the fault lies partly with Captain Johnston (who really did not know where he was going anyway), but mostly with Stuart—who is not even there! Forgotten in all of this is the fact that earlier that morning Lafayette McLaws had requested permission to scout the route of march to avoid precisely what happened to the 1st Corps column. But Longstreet had forbidden McLaws to leave his division, and now paid the price of his truculence. The entire column of some 14,000 men was forced to countermarch nearly to the point where the march had begun, to use a different route.

Around 3 p.m. the head of the 1st Corps arrived in the vicinity of the Pitzer School House, approximately one-half mile west of Seminary Ridge. It had taken three hours to move about one and one-half miles. At the school house McLaws' Division turned onto the Millerstown Road and began marching east toward Seminary Ridge. As Shaara relates, he finds a surprise when he arrives on the ridge. In his front, the Peach Orchard, which should have had no enemy troops in its vicinity, is crawling with Federal soldiers, whose lines extend as far to the right and left as the ground will permit seeing. In the book, McLaws informs Longstreet of this development and the 1st Corps commander calmly and competently takes charge and attempts to make the best of a bad situation. But, according to McLaws, the real Longstreet did not

14

respond as well to this development. When McLaws sent word back to Longstreet that the enemy occupied the Peach Orchard in force, and that he was not on the flank of the Union army, Longstreet, who had not yet even looked at the Union line, sent a reply that "he was satisfied there was a small force of the enemy in front," and that McLaws should "proceed at once to the assault." Some minutes later, when Longstreet did not hear McLaws' artillery in action, he sent Major Osmun Latrobe of headquarters staff to investigate the cause of the delay. McLaws explained to Latrobe that he would attack, but he had to make careful preparations due to the strength of the Union position. Latrobe repeated Longstreet's directive to attack at once. At the last moment, when McLaws was ready to signal the attack, Longstreet—who apparently had been convinced that the enemy was in front in strength—rode up and ordered McLaws to delay his assault until Hood could move up and attack.[21] Longstreet's conduct infuriated McLaws. He wrote his wife after the battle:

> General Longstreet is to blame for not reconnoitering the ground, and for persisting in ordering the assault when his errors were discovered. During the engagement he was very excited giving contrary orders to everyone, and was exceedingly overbearing. I consider him a humbug—a man of small capacity, very obstinate, not at all chivalrous, exceedingly conceited, and totally selfish. If I can it is my intentions to get away from his command.

Maj. Gen. John B. Hood

These were strong words from a man who had carried a high opinion of Longstreet into the engagement at Gettysburg.[22]

In his admiration for Longstreet, Shaara attempts to shift the responsibility of the 1st Corps trials and tribulations on July 2 to others' shoulders. First it is Lee, whose unimaginative battle plan puts Longstreet at a disadvantage. Then it is Captain Johnston, who does not know the roads and leads the 1st Corps column awry. Finally, it is Stuart, who by his absence leaves the army stumbling blindly about. Longstreet is blameless—the good soldier caught up in a bad situation. The truth is that Longstreet must assume much of the accountability for what befell his corps on July 2. As the army commander, Lee had the right to expect his subordinates to attempt to execute his orders with resourcefulness and initiative. Longstreet evidenced little of either quality on the 2nd. He deliberately delayed his movements until given a direct order to march. When he found the enemy in an unexpected position he made no effort to improvise. Instead he stubbornly executed Lee's orders to attack "up the Emmitsburg Road" even though those orders were based upon a reconnaissance that was nearly ten hours old by the time Longstreet had arrived on Seminary Ridge. In an interesting comparison, at the Battle of Chancellorsville when "Stonewall" Jackson was directed to conduct a demanding flank march, he came upon where Lee believed the Union flank to rest, discovered Lee's information to be erroneous, and pushed until he had located the enemy flank. The rest is history.

Longstreet did not lose the Battle of Gettysburg. As army commander, Lee bears the principal burden for the Confederate Army. But the performance of the Longstreet of history differs largely from the Longstreet of the pages of *The Killer Angels*. Moxley Sorrel, Longstreet's chief of staff, and a man who remained on close terms with his former commander throughout his life, admitted that on July 2 "there was apparent apathy in his movements. They lacked the fire and point of his usual bearing on the battlefield."[23]

❖ ❖ ❖

One of the most memorable passages in *The Killer Angels* is the story of Joshua Chamberlain and the 20th Maine on Little Round Top. Thanks to Shaara's book and the 1993 film *Gettysburg*, Chamberlain has gained enormous popularity. His regiment's stand on Little Round Top—a magnificent feat of arms—has been lionized until it has assumed Arthurian proportions. Chamberlain is deserving of great credit. He fought with bravery, skill, tenacity, and cunning to win a crucial engagement, but he did not stand off the enemy alone. He was not the only hero on Little Round Top that hot July 2 afternoon, and Chamberlain would have been the first to admit it. But because Shaara presents the events at Little Round Top through Chamberlain's eyes, his story is the only one the reader comes to know.

Col. Strong Vincent

Chamberlain's brigade commander, Colonel Strong Vincent, briefly appears for several pages and then is gone. Shaara does not dwell upon Vincent, but he played a vital role in the battle for Little Round Top. When Vincent's Brigade arrived in the battle area on July 2, Longstreet's artillery had already opened fire upon Sickles' advanced line, and the Confederate infantry was preparing to attack. Brigadier General James Barnes, commanding the division to which Vincent's Brigade belonged, halted his division and rode forward to find someone who could tell him where to place his command. Meanwhile, the Chief Engineer of the Army of the Potomac, Brigadier General Gouvernor K. Warren, had discovered that Little Round Top was unoccupied by Union troops. He sent a courier galloping to Major General George Sykes, commanding the 5th Army Corps, and requested a brigade of infantry to occupy the hill. Sykes agreed to provide the infantry and sent a staff officer with an order to Barnes to detach one of his three brigades and send it to Little Round Top. But Barnes was absent, reconnoitering a position for his division. Sykes' staff officer encountered Vincent instead, who convinced him to disclose Sykes' orders to Barnes. Without a moment's hesitation Vincent took it upon himself to detach his brigade and lead it to Little Round Top.[24]

In the novel, Vincent rides along with his brigade as they march to their destiny on the rock strewn slopes of Little Round Top. In reality, Vincent left Colonel James Rice of the 44th New York to conduct the march. He rode ahead to the summit of the hill with his orderly, Oliver Norton, in order to scout the ground and determine where best to place his regiments. All but forgotten in the telling of Chamberlain's magnificent stand is the fact that Vincent picked the ground the 20th Maine defended. His good judgement in selecting where to place his regiments and his careful deployment of them played no small part in the ability of his men to successfully defend the hill against repeated Confederate attacks.

Unlike Chamberlain, Vincent did not live to tell his tale. He fell mortally wounded while trying to rally elements of the 16th Michigan, located on the extreme right flank of the brigade. Another hero on that hill died near Vincent. Colonel Patrick O'Rorke, commander of the 140th New York Infantry, was number one in the class of 1861 at West Point. The young Irishman had a promising future before him. But fate placed his regiment marching over the northern shoulder of Little Round Top at the moment Vincent's right flank began to crumble. General Warren spurred down the hill and asked O'Rorke to bring his regiment to Vincent's aid. O'Rorke's brigade commander, Brigadier General Stephen Weed, had ridden ahead and was not available for consultation. O'Rorke did not hesitate in his answer to Warren, and led his regiment up the rocky slopes. They reached the summit at the critical moment when Vincent's right flank was crumbling under Confederate attack, and O'Rorke led his men

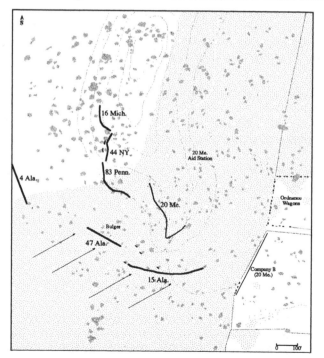

Map of Little Round Top and the assault on Vincent's Brigade.

Col. Patrick O'Rorke

down the slope. A bullet passed through his neck and he died instantly. But his regiment drove the Confederate attackers back and restored the right flank of Vincent's line.[25]

While Vincent and O'Rorke gave up their lives to hold the right of the Union line on Little Round Top, the 20th Maine engaged in a desperate battle to defend the left of the line. The battle ultimately reached a critical point; ammunition was low in the 20th Maine and casualties were heavy. It was a dramatic moment, but the actual conflict differed in some particulars from Shaara's version. For instance, acting Major Ellis Spear recalled he had no contact with Chamberlain after the left flank of the 20th Maine had been refused. And, he claimed, his companies did not run out of ammunition. The ammunition shortage occurred on the right and center of the regiment, where Chamberlain was. The story of Lieutenant Holman Melcher of Company F is accurate. He approached Chamberlain and requested permission to advance his line to cover the wounded lying in front of the line (the 20th's center had been pushed back a short distance and some of the wounded were left between the opposing lines). Melcher though, was not a "gaunt boy with buck teeth." He was handsome and a natural leader. Elisha Coan, a member of the color guard of the 20th Maine, recalled Melcher's request to Chamberlain: "Lt. Melcher conceived the idea of advancing the colors so that our line would cover our wounded & dead so that they could be removed to the rear and he asked Col. C. for the privilege of advancing his Company for that purpose."

Lt. Holman Melcher

Melcher's request, coupled with reports from company officers that ammunition had given out, caused Chamberlain to make his bold decision to launch a bayonet charge.[25]

In the novel Chamberlain gathers with Spear, Kilrain, and Melcher to explain his plan to charge with bayonets while executing a right wheel forward, a movement whereby a unit swings like a gate to the right. Lieutenant Melcher innocently pipes up to ask what a right wheel forward is. Of course the real Lieutenant Melcher knew exactly what a right wheel forward was and how to execute it. The 20th Maine had been in the service for nearly one year and had been well drilled in military tactics. Everyone in the regiment knew how to execute a right wheel forward. Yet, there is some question whether Chamberlain ordered a right wheel forward or if the veterans of the 20th Maine carried one out instinctively. Chamberlain reported that he gave one command after his brief interchange with Lieutenant Melcher over advancing the line to retrieve the wounded. He shouted "bayonets!" "It was vain to order 'forward,'" Chamberlain wrote later. "No mortal could have heard it in the mighty hosanna that was winging the sky. Nor would he wait to hear." Howard L. Prince, the Quartermaster Sergeant of the regiment, wrote: "Col.

Maj. Ellis Spear

Chamberlain does not know whether he ever finished that order. In an instant, less time than has been required to tell it, Lt. Melcher has sprung ahead of the line, the colors are advancing, and with one wild rush the devoted regiment hurls itself down the ledge into the midst of the gray lines, not thirty paces distant." On the left flank of the 20th Maine, Ellis Spear recalled:

> Suddenly, in the midst of the noise of musketry, I heard a shout on the center, of "forward" and saw the line and colors began to move. I had received no orders, other than to hold the left and guard the flank and did not understand the meaning of the movement. But there was not time to seek explanation...so there was nothing else but move the left so I also shouted "forward" and we all joined in the shout, and movement, and went in a rush down the slope and over the scattered men of the enemy....[26]

However, Spear related that his companies advanced forward, or due east, in pursuit of fleeing Confederates. Their movements did not conform to those of the center and right of the regiment. Spear's companies, at least, did not perform a right wheel forward.[27]

On the third day of the battle, Shaara shifts Chamberlain's 20th Maine to Cemetery Ridge, the center of the Army of the Potomac's position. This is pure fiction. The 20th Maine moved on July 3 from Big Round Top to a ridge running north from Little Round Top, where today the New Jersey Brigade has a monument marking their position—a good three-quarters of a mile from the Clump of Trees on Cemetery Ridge. But Shaara wanted Chamberlain to be at the center of the action on July 3 and took literary license to place him there.

In his travels in the novel, Chamberlain sees Meade, the army commander, and does not "know what to think of him." Actually, Chamberlain probably knew "what to think of him" more than most men in the army. Meade had been commander of the 5th Corps, which the 20th Maine belonged to, for several months before assuming command of the army. Soon after seeing Meade, Chamberlain encounters Lieutenant Frank Haskall, an aide to General John Gibbon of the 2nd Corps. Haskall is a famous personality of the battle because he authored a lengthy account of the battle to his brother which was subsequently published, and has since become a Harvard Classic. The fact is, Chamberlain never met Frank Haskall on the Gettysburg battlefield, and even if he did, Haskall would not have recognized his name. While Chamberlain's gallant action on Little Round Top had been made known to the 5th Corps Commander General George Sykes, his heroics were not known outside of the 5th Corps and would not be for some months after the battle. It is important to keep Joshua Chamberlain in the proper perspective. Years after the battle was over and veterans had an opportunity to study the battle they had participated in, the heroics of the 20th Maine and their gallant colonel became relatively well known. But in July, 1863, outside of Chamberlain's own 5th Corps, his actions on Little Round Top were not well known. And even if they had been, men from other army corps might not have been impressed, for every corps in the army, except the 6th Corps, had participated in severe fighting and contributed their own fair share of heroes.[28]

❖ ❖ ❖

"Pickett's Charge" is the most famous action of the Battle of Gettysburg. For several of Shaara's characters it is the climatic moment of the battle—the final scene in a tragedy of epic proportions. In Shaara's version, the plan to launch the attack comes to a weary General Lee like a dream that plays itself out in his mind. He has struck both flanks of the Union army; therefore, he concludes that the center must be weak. Thus, the center is where he will strike with overwhelming force, while Stuart and his cavalry are dispatched to penetrate the enemy rear. Having made his plan he turns to God in prayer where he finds an exhilarating release from the bonds of his deadly command decision. It is a moving passage. Yet, as believable as Shaara's accounting may be, the real General Lee arrived at an entirely different decision the night of July 2.

The reports received by Lee during the early evening and night of July 2 indicated that while the day's attacks had not been as successful as hoped for, they had nevertheless inflicted great damage upon the Union army and gained ground. From Lee's perspective, he was winning the battle. Victory on July 2 had slipped through his grasp only because his army had failed to coordinate its attacks (principally Ewell had not moved in concert with Longstreet's attack). Lee's original plan for July 3 did not envision an attack upon the Union center. Instead he intended that Longstreet and Ewell would simultaneously assail the Union flanks from the ground won on July 2. "The general plan was unchanged," wrote Lee in his report. "Longstreet, re-enforced by Pickett's three brigades, ...was ordered to attack the next morning, and Ewell was directed to assail the enemy's right at the same time." Stuart's cavalry would attempt to penetrate to the Union rear in order to cut communications and create a diversion that Meade might find disconcerting. This was Lee's plan. Pickett's Charge did not exist. But Lee did not transmit his orders in writing. They were delivered verbally and this led to a grave misunderstanding. And, the Union army did not sit meekly and await a renewal of the Confederate attack. They took action, causing further disruption to Lee's plans.[29]

The Confederate attack was scheduled to open at daylight. But at dawn on July 3 the Confederate infantry poised to attack the remaining Union positions on Culp's Hill was subjected to a furious bombardment by Union artillery of the 12th Corps. This barrage was planned to precede an infantry attack to drive Ewell's Confederates off. Instead it caused nervous soldiers on both sides to open fire, and soon a tremendous musketry battle exploded. With the battle already joined on the Union right, Lee rode to Longstreet's headquarters to see how his senior corps commander's preparations were progressing. In contrast to *The Killer Angels*, Lee and Longstreet did not meet on the night of July 2. Longstreet had sent a staff officer to Lee to report on the day's operations. To his astonishment Lee discovered that Longstreet had made no preparations to attack, but instead was drawing up orders to move his corps around Big Round Top in order to turn the flank of the Union army. Either Longstreet had misunderstood, or he had taken a liberal interpretation of his orders. Whichever, his unauthorized flanking movement was not what Lee had intended.[30]

With Longstreet unprepared to open his corps attack and Ewell already engaged, Lee was forced to develop an entirely new plan for the day. Longstreet adamantly opposed a renewal of the attack upon the strong Union left—an opinion he would have done well to have voiced in person to Lee the night before. Lee agreed with Longstreet's argument but refused to be dissuaded from his determination to strike the enemy. Instead, he settled upon a huge attack upon the Union center on Cemetery Ridge. He did not arrive at this decision by impulse, or because he was tired, or had dreamed it up, as Shaara might imply. He decided upon it for sound reasons that he firmly believed would work and win his army victory. The attack that Lee envisioned and placed under Longstreet's command would open with the largest concentrated artillery bombardment ever employed in a North American land battle. Once the bombardment had silenced the Union artillery, two and one-half divisions of infantry; Pickett's, Pettigrew's and half of Trimble's, slightly over 12,000 men, would advance, close with the Union infantry defenders and overwhelm them, breaching the center of the Union army. The plan entailed enormous risks, but few plans in war do not. It was a gamble for victory. A similar frontal attack had won the bloody Battle of Solferino in Italy for the French in 1859 and successfully ended their war against Austria. Fifty years earlier, Napoleon's Grande Armee broke the Austrian center at Wagram with a massive frontal assault and won a great victory for France. Lee gambled that his army, which he believed was superior to the Union army in everything except numbers, could duplicate the French successes at Wagram and Solferino.

As for Longstreet, Shaara correctly develops the gloom that settled upon the 1st Corps commander. He opposed the attack and had little faith in its success. By his own account he opposed the attack more strenuously with Lee than Shaara describes in *The Killer Angels*. But Lee was determined, and Longstreet was obliged to follow orders. In the novel Longstreet instructs Lieutenant Colonel Edward P. Alexander, in temporary command of the 1st Corps artillery on July 3, to fire upon the Union battery on Little Round Top with "everything you have." Longstreet also advises Alexander that he must observe the effect of the artillery fire upon the Union line. "I'll rely on your judgement," states Longstreet, apparently to determine when is the most opportune moment to send the infantry attack forward.[31]

The principal target of Alexander's artillery was not Little Round Top, as Shaara's Longstreet seems to imply, but the Union artillery on Cemetery Ridge, where the infantry attack would strike. It was necessary to silence or drive off these Union guns to allow the Confederate infantry to cross the one mile of open ground without suffering crippling losses. Only a very small number of Alexander's available guns were dedicated to firing upon the Union battery on Little Round Top. Although it was recognized that this battery could cause trouble for the Confederate infantry advance, the Union guns on Cemetery Ridge were of more importance.

As for Longstreet's reliance upon Alexander's judgement to determine when to order the infantry forward, there is truth to this, but the story is more complicated and less complimentary to General Longstreet than the one Shaara tells. Alexander's initial orders from Longstreet were to "drive off or greatly demoralize" the Union artillery, and to advance such artillery as was possible to support the infantry when it advanced. Soon before the pre-attack artillery bombardment commenced, Alexander received a note from Longstreet. It read:

Col. Edward P. Alexander

Colonel. If the artillery fire does not have the effect to drive off the enemy, or greatly demoralize him, so as to make our efforts pretty certain, I would prefer that you should not advise Gen. Pickett to make the charge. I shall rely a great deal on your good judgement to determine the matter & shall expect you to let Gen. Pickett know when the moment offers.[32]

"This presented the whole business to me in a new light," wrote Alexander. Longstreet was not merely relying upon Alexander's judgement for advice - he was placing the entire burden of deciding whether the attack should go forward or not upon the shoulders of a 28 year old lieutenant colonel! Alexander responded with a note which politely attempted to point out that the decision to make, or not make, the attack belonged to Longstreet. But Longstreet's reply to this note left the burden of determining the moment that Pickett should advance upon Alexander. Alexander recalled that Brigadier General A. R. Wright, an infantry brigade commander who was present with him, read Longstreet's note and said, "He has put the responsibility back upon you." "I had tried to avoid the responsibility of the decision, but in vain," recalled

Alexander. It was an odd episode and did not reflect well upon Longstreet. He later attempted to explain his actions, writing: "I still desired to save my men, and felt that if the artillery did not have the desired effect, I would be justified in holding Pickett off."[33]

The objective of Pickett's Charge is frequently misunderstood by students of Gettysburg, and Shaara reinforces a common misconception on this point. On three occasions in the novel the "clump of trees" on Cemetery Ridge is pointed out as the objective of the attack upon which "all fifteen thousand" men will concentrate. The "clump of trees" was not an objective of the attack and it was never Lee's intention to concentrate so many men upon such a small area. Possession of the trees meant absolutely nothing. The "clump of trees" figured into the planning because they were situated near the center of the Cemetery Ridge position and could serve as a discernable topographical feature toward which the assaulting troops could guide their movements. The attack would strike the Union Cemetery Ridge line along a front of nearly one-half mile, not "a hundred yards wide" section of stone wall, as Shaara's Longstreet believes. This landmark status was the sole importance of the trees to Pickett's Charge. Their only other significance resulted when some of Pickett's men penetrated as far as the trees at the climax of the attack. This earned the trees the designation in the postwar period as the "High Water Mark" of Pickett's Charge and the Confederacy.

❖ ❖ ❖

Perhaps the most controversial passage of *The Killer Angels* is Shaara's depiction of Lee, as seen by Longstreet after the repulse of Pickett's Charge. Shaara's Lee, apparently greatly shaken by the disastrous result of the attack, rides among his retreating soldiers to repeatedly apologize that "it is all my fault," that the attack has failed. Yet, there is no inspiration or fire in Shaara's Lee. He is merely an old man whose efforts to rally his soldiers are pathetic.[34]

Robert E. Lee's actions following the repulse of Pickett's Charge must rank as one of his most sublime examples of leadership, and stand in sharp contrast to Shaara's depiction of him. Disaster stared Lee in the face after the failure of the attack, a disaster of his own making. He had ordered the attack. He had believed it would succeed over the objections of his senior lieutenant. And it had failed at a terrible price in human suffering. Had Lee recoiled from confronting the reality of the disaster it would have been understandable. The enormity of it all was so great that few people could have borne it or faced it. Yet Lee, despite his own personal anguish, confronted the consequences of his actions. Arthur Freemantle, the British observer with the Army of Northern Virginia, observed his actions and recorded them in his diary:

> If Longstreet's conduct was admirable, that of General Lee was perfectly sublime. He was engaged in rallying and in encouraging the

A portion of Paul Philippoteaux's Gettysburg Cyclorama illustrating Pickett's Charge and the High Tide of the Confederacy.

Brig. Gen. Lewis A. Armistead.

27

broken troops...His face which is always placid and cheerful, did not show the slightest disappointment, care, or annoyance, and he was addressing to every soldier he met a few words of encouragement...

He spoke to all the wounded men that passed him, and the slightly wounded he exhorted "to bind up [their] hurts and take up a musket" in this emergency. Very few failed to answer his appeal, and I saw many badly wounded men take off their hats and cheer him. He said to me, "this has been a sad day for us, Colonel - a sad day; but we can't expect always to gain victories."...

I saw General Willcox (an officer who wears a short round jacket and a battered straw hat) come up to him, and explain, almost crying, the state of his brigade. General Lee immediately shook hands with him and said cheerfully, "Never mind, General, all this has been MY fault—it is I that have lost this fight, and you must help me out of it in the best way you can."...

In this manner I saw General Lee encourage and reanimate his somewhat dispirited troops, and magnanimously take upon his own shoulders the whole weight of the repulse. It was impossible to look at him or listen to him without feeling the strongest admiration, and I never saw any man fail him except the man in the ditch.[35]

Lee shouldered the entire responsibility for the failure of Pickett's Charge and for the defeat at Gettysburg. He never deviated from this stand for the rest of his life. Historians may dispute and question his tactics at Gettysburg, but none will question his courage, leadership, and selfless actions when defeat and disaster stared him in the face on July 3, 1863.

THE PEOPLE

What happened to the men of Shaara's novel after Gettysburg? The war continued. In fact, 1864 would be the bloodiest year of the war and bring Union morale to the brink of collapse. Not until April 1865 would Robert E. Lee's Army of Northern Virginia surrender and bring about the collapse of the Confederacy.

ROBERT E. LEE

Following Gettysburg, Lee submitted his resignation to Confederate President Jefferson Davis. It was refused; the South had no one who could replace Lee. He withdrew his army south of the Rapidan River in Virginia where it could reorganize and recover from the massive casualties suffered at Gettysburg. Between 22,000 and 28,000 soldiers had been killed, wounded, or captured. Thousands more had deserted during the retreat from Pennsylvania. Fortunately for Lee, the Union Army of the Potomac had also suffered dreadful casualties at Gettysburg and was content to leave the Confederates alone.

Events elsewhere in the country did not permit Lee a long respite. Vicksburg, Mississippi had fallen to the Union forces under Ulysses S. Grant on July 4, 1863, and the Federal army of Major General William S. Rosecrans had outmaneuvered Braxton Bragg's Confederate Army of Tennessee and captured the strategically important city of Chattanooga, Tennessee. The setbacks of the summer of 1863 had thrown the Confederacy on the defensive everywhere. To retrieve this situation, an offensive designed to defeat Rosecrans' army and regain Tennessee was planned. Lee agreed to detach Longstreet with Hood's and McLaws' Divisions to reinforce the Army of Tennessee. They departed in early September to take part in the Confederate victory at Chickamauga, Georgia on September 19 and 20, 1863.

With Longstreet gone, Lee had perhaps 50,000 effective soldiers. Through the fall of 1863 he sparred with Meade's Army of the Potomac in northern Virginia at Bristoe Station and Mine Run, but both armies avoided committing to a general battle. The spring of 1864 brought Ulysses S. Grant to command of all Union forces. Grant believed that if Lee and the Army of Northern Virginia could be destroyed, the entire rebellion would collapse. It had been the consistent success of that army that gave the Confederacy hope that its independence might be won. Therefore, although Grant directed the opera-

29

tions of all Union armies throughout the country, he placed his headquarters in the field with General George G. Meade and the Army of the Potomac, to personally direct the offensive against Lee.

On May 4, 1864, Grant led an army of nearly 116,000 men into the Wilderness, a tract of thick, almost impenetrable forest west of Fredericksburg, Virginia. Lee's forces numbered 64,000, including Longstreet who had returned from the western theater. Lee struck Grant's columns before they could debouch into the more open country to the south and a furious battle developed. At one point when some of Lee's forces broke and disaster threatened, Lee placed himself to personally lead a counterattack by the Texas Brigade of Longstreet's Corps. The soldiers refused to attack unless Lee went to safety in the rear. He did, reluctantly, prompting one soldier to remark, "I would charge hell itself for that old man." The battle swung in favor of the Army of Northern Virginia, but Grant was unlike any general Lee had faced in the eastern theater of the war. Defeat did not discourage him. He simply ordered a movement to the east, in the hopes that he could get between Lee and Richmond. Lee managed to move swiftly enough to bar Grant's path at Spotsylvania Court House. Here, another bloody battle raged from May 9 to May 18. This was a new kind of war. Previously, the two armies would come together, a great battle of one to three days would ensue, then one (usually the Federal army) would withdraw to refit and reorganize before attempting another campaign. Grant never disengaged, unless it was to attempt to outmaneuver the enemy; he simply bored ahead. The armies were in contact every day. Digging in became standard policy in both armies. The pressure and tension were immense.[1]

The campaign placed a tremendous strain upon Lee. Longstreet fell wounded in the Wilderness and "Jeb" Stuart was mortally wounded at Yellow Tavern on May 11. The loss of these officers and many more compelled Lee to take a more active role in directing tactical operations in the field than ever before. His health suffered, yet he continued to perform brilliantly.

Following the inconclusive fighting at Spotsylvania Court House, Grant moved east to the North Anna River, where Lee again checked him. Grant simply moved east again, this time to Cold Harbor, where he attacked and suffered a terrible repulse. But Lee could not exploit his victory. His army had suffered heavy losses in the spring campaign and lacked the strength to go over to the offensive. Grant moved again, this time conducting a daring crossing of the James River to strike a blow at Petersburg, Virginia, which in all likelihood would have ended the war. But, although Grant's movement fooled Lee, his exhausted troops were unable to exploit their opportunity and the effort to capture Petersburg failed. Lee moved his army into the fortifications around Richmond and Petersburg and the two armies settled into a grim siege warfare that ground on through the fall and into the winter.

By the spring of 1865, Lee's weakened army stretched along a front of more than twenty miles. On March 31 Union forces captured Five Forks, a strategic road junction southwest of Petersburg. Two days later, April 2, Grant's forces broke Lee's lines in several places, forcing Lee to evacuate Richmond and Petersburg and attempt to escape to the west. Grant pursued and brought Lee to bay at Appomattox Court House. Convinced of the hopelessness of his situation, Lee agreed to surrender. He met Grant at the McLean House in the village of Appomattox Court House on April 9, 1865. Horace Porter, an officer on Grant's staff, recalled Lee as he emerged from his historic meeting with Grant:

> Lee signaled to his orderly to bring up his horse, and while the animal was being bridled the general stood on the lowest step and gazed sadly in the direction of the valley beyond where his army lay—now an army of prisoners. He smote his hands together a number of times in an absent sort of way; he seemed not to see the group of Union officers in the yard who rose respectfully at his approach, and appeared unconscious of everything about him. All appreciated the sadness that overwhelmed him, and he had the personal sympathy of every one who beheld him at this supreme moment of trial.[2]

Lee met his defeat with dignity and honor. He had battled with skill and tenacity for the Confederacy. Now that it was dead he set an example of leadership to the vanquished South by encouraging the people to recognize the United States as their country and to work towards healing the bitter wounds opened by the war. In Lee's mind the war was over and it was time for the South to bury their bitterness and rebuild their shattered states. He told a friend, "Now more than at any other time, Virginia and every other state in the South needs us. We must try and, with as little delay as possible, to go to work to build up their prosperity."[3]

In the fall of 1865 he accepted the position of president of Washington College in Lexington, Virginia. As president, Lee put into practice his advice to the South to put the past behind and meet the needs of the present and future. He planned a restructuring of the curriculum, which previous to his arrival had taught Greek, Latin, Natural Philosophy, Mathematics and Moral Philosophy, to better prepare the youth of the South to meet the challenges of the future. He planned a group of scientific schools, added Spanish to the foreign language training, developed a school of commerce and agriculture, and a school of law, among other advanced ideas. The New York *Herald* proclaimed that Lee's ideas on education were "likely to make as great an impression upon our old fogey schools and colleges as [General Lee] did in military tactics upon our old fogey commanders in the palmy days of the rebellion."[4]

Lee did not live to see his ideas on education implemented. Heart disease, which had plagued him since 1863, claimed his life on October 12, 1870. He is buried in Lexington, Virginia.

JAMES LONGSTREET

In early September, 1863, Longstreet accompanied the divisions of Hood and McLaws of his 1st Corps on a long rail journey west to reinforce General Braxton Bragg's Army of Tennessee, then positioned in northern Georgia. Longstreet reached Ringgold, Georgia, on September 19, the first day of the Battle of Chickamauga. Bragg assigned Longstreet to command of the "left wing" of the army—a force of 22,000 men. The battle resumed on September 20, and developed into a bloody, confused combat in the thickly wooded terrain. But at about mid-day, Longstreet's wing struck the Union line at a vulnerable point and broke it open in furious fighting. The result of the day's fighting was a Confederate victory that sent the Union army reeling back to Chattanooga in retreat.

The Army of Tennessee was an unhappy army. Bragg, an irascible and unpleasant fellow, fell into rancorous bickering with his senior generals, including Longstreet, who detested him. The relations between these two generals degenerated until in early November, 1863, Longstreet was detached

with McLaws and Hood (now under Evander Law) on an independent operation to seize Knoxville, Tennessee. Knoxville was defended by Union forces under General Ambrose Burnside, who had encircled the city with fortifications. Longstreet came up against these on November 11, and on November 29 launched an attack with part of McLaws' and Hood's Divisions that resulted in the most complete repulse suffered by any troops of the Army of Northern Virginia during the war. The campaign ended in failure and Longstreet, revealing an ugly side of his person, sought to shift the blame to others' shoulders. He relieved Generals Lafayette McLaws and Jerome Robertson, both officers of long standing in Longstreet's Corps. Court-martial charges were preferred against McLaws for the failure of the November 29 assault, and other disharmony and bickering among the officer corps of his command developed.[5] It was an unhappy and unproductive winter.

In April 1864 Longstreet's command was transferred back to Virginia in preparation for the anticipated Union spring offensive. Although Longstreet had coveted an independent command, the experience in Tennessee had been an unpleasant and embarrassing one, and he told one staff officer "he preferred being under General Lee, as it relieved him of responsibility and assured confidence."[6]

On May 6, 1864, the second day of the Battle of the Wilderness, Longstreet's Corps arrived on the field at a critical point and drove the Federal troops back. But, at this moment of success Longstreet was accidently fired upon by his own men and severely wounded. He returned to Georgia to recover and did not rejoin the army until October 1864. Through the long, dismal winter of trench warfare to the surrender at Appomattox Court House,

Lee relied heavily upon Longstreet to help hold the army together and to keep the Federal forces in check.

Following the war, Longstreet relocated to New Orleans where he engaged in the cotton business and enjoyed considerable financial success. Like Lee, he advocated a moderate view toward the federal government and reconstruction policies. But unlike Lee, who did not air his views in public, Longstreet released a letter to the New Orleans press that encouraged the South to cooperate with the Republicans. Instead, it caused outrage. Southerners held the Republican party largely responsible for everything that had befallen them. To have a former distinguished general of the Confederate army advocate reconciliation with them was unthinkable. But Longstreet did more than simply express his views in the press; he also joined the Republican Party. This act the South did not forgive. He was labeled a Judas and harshly condemned, even by former friends and comrades.

Longstreet's reputation suffered further damage during the 1870s and 1880s when his performance at Gettysburg was assailed by former Confederate officers Jubal Early and William N. Pendleton. Stung by their attacks, Longstreet countered with his own version of the battle, but readers found his graceless effort arrogant and self-serving. In 1895 his memoirs, titled *From Manassas to Appomattox* were published. They did little to improve his tarnished reputation, perceived by readers as the account of a vain, disloyal subordinate. He freely and sometimes harshly criticized Lee and Jackson, which moved Edward P. Alexander to write, "Longstreet's great mistake was not in the war, but in some of his awkward and apparently bitter criticisms of Gen. Lee."[7]

Despite his unpopularity in much of the postwar South, and with many ex-Confederate officers, Longstreet's connections with the Republican party managed to land him several government appointments. He served as postmaster at Gainesville, Georgia in 1879, U. S. Minister to Turkey in 1880, and in 1897 President William McKinley appointed him U. S. Commissioner of Railroads. Throughout the last years of his life he continued to be vilified by his numerous enemies for his criticisms of Lee and alleged failures at Gettysburg. He died in Gainesville, Georgia on January 2, 1904.

The image of James Longstreet today is heavily influenced by the writings of Douglas Southal Freeman, the author of the multi-volume works *R. E. Lee* and *Lee's Lieutenants*, written in the 1930s and 1940s, respectively. Both are classic works on the Army of Northern Virginia and are still widely read. Freeman embraced the anti-Longstreet faction and his portrayal of the general was unfavorable and unbalanced, particularly in dealing with Longstreet at Gettysburg. But Freeman's critical portrait of Longstreet was mild compared to Clifford Dowdey, a Virginia newspaperman and novelist who authored several highly acclaimed books on Lee and the Army of Northern Virginia during the 1950s and early 1960s. Dowdey attacked Longstreet at every opportunity and further solidified the image of the general that had emerged in the postwar South.

Arriving at a balanced opinion of James Longstreet is difficult. He was a controversial man, even during the Civil War. Recent scholarship, such as Jeffry Wert's book, *General James Longstreet: The Confederacy's Most Controversial Soldier, A Biography*, and William Garrett Piston's biography, although sympathetic to Longstreet, offer a more reasonable assessment of the man and soldier.

GEORGE E. PICKETT

Gettysburg was George Pickett's moment of glory, but it would be a moment that haunted him the rest of his days. To some officers and men in the army it seemed odd that Pickett had emerged unscathed when so many of the officers in his division had been cut down. Pickett was sensitive to this and later told an officer in his division, "that on the day after the battle he felt that he would have no right to resent the insult if someone should accuse him of cowardice, because he was not among the killed, wounded or captured."[8]

Following the battle, Pickett's shattered division was assigned to guarding the Union prisoners from the battle—a duty that mortified Pickett. His division was subsequently reassigned to the Department of Virginia and North Carolina, a large area that extended from south of Richmond to eastern North Carolina. He organized an effort to recapture New Berne, North Carolina in February 1864 that ended unsuccessfully. In May 1864 he distinguished himself in the successful effort to stop the advance of Union General Benjamin Butler's forces at Bermuda Hundred, Virginia. But the strain upon Pickett left him mentally and physically exhausted and he was relieved of duty to recover. He returned to his command in June 1864, but did little to distinguish himself during the siege of Richmond and Petersburg. Then, in the last dark days of the war he suddenly was thrust into a critical position.

On March 30, 1865, Lee ordered Pickett to take his division to Five Forks, a crucial road junction southwest of Petersburg that guarded the Southside Railroad, the lifeline of Lee's army. On April 1, with misplaced confidence that he would not be attacked by Union infantry that day, Pickett rode two miles to the rear to enjoy a shad-bake with generals Fitz Lee and Thomas Rosser. During his absence, Pickett's command was attacked by the Union forces under General Philip Sheridan and crushed. The Federals seized the Southside Railroad and the next day Lee's army abandoned Petersburg and Richmond and retreated west. On April 8, 1865, Lee relieved Pickett of duty with the army.

Pickett's postwar career was an unhappy one. He fled to Canada after the war to escape possible prosecution for an incident during his tenure in the Department of Virginia and North Carolina. In February 1864 twenty-two prisoners from the 2nd U. S. North Carolina Volunteers who were accused of being deserters from the Confederate army, were hung by Pickett's orders. Ulysses S. Grant intervened on Pickett's behalf and he was able to return to the United States in 1866. He took up residence in Norfolk, Virginia, where he was an insurance agent. Pickett never truly recovered from the war. The disaster at Five Forks and his relief from command in the last days of the war left him embittered, particularly towards Lee. Once, in 1870, John Singleton Mosby, the great Confederate guerrilla fighter, brought Lee and Pickett together in the hope that they might mend the wounds the war had wrought upon their relationship. But both men were tense and uncommunicative. As Mosby led Pickett away from the unsuccessful attempt at reconciliation, Pickett cried out, loud enough for Lee to hear, "That man sacrificed my division at Gettysburg."[9]

Pickett died July 30, 1875, at age 50. He is buried in Hollywood Cemetery in Richmond, Virginia.

J. E. B. STUART

Stuart was stung by the criticism he received at the hands of the Southern press following the Confederate defeat at Gettysburg. He attempted to cover his errors and retrieve his lost prestige by releasing a campaign report that vindicated his actions. But in his own official report of the campaign Lee wrote that "the movements of the army preceding the battle of Gettysburg had been much embarrassed by the absence of the cavalry," which for Lee, was harsh censure of Stuart's performance.[10]

During the fall campaigns of 1863 Stuart returned to his old form, serving the army efficiently and effectively. But the quality and numbers of his cavalry were declining due to shortages in manpower and horses, while the Union cavalry grew more numerous and aggressive.

In the opening stages of Grant's Overland Campaign in the spring of 1864, Stuart encountered a new and deadly Union adversary in Philip H. Sheridan, commander of the Army of the Potomac's Cavalry Corps. Following skirmishing in the opening stages of the Battle of the Wilderness, Stuart discovered that Sheridan had led his 10,000 cavalry troopers on a raid toward Richmond. Stuart eventually brought Sheridan to bay at Yellow Tavern, north of Richmond, on May 11, where their two forces clashed. In the course of the fighting a dismounted Union trooper shot Stuart in the abdomen with a pistol

He died on the evening of May 12 from the effects of his wound. As he was being helped from the field he revealed his indomitable spirit when he shouted to some retreating troopers: "Go back, go back and do your duty, as I have done mine, and our country will be safe. Go back, go back! I had rather die than be whipped."[11]

Perhaps the best tribute to Stuart's abilities and contribution to the Army of Northern Virginia was offered by Lee, who, when he learned of his cavalry commander's death, exclaimed: "He never brought me a piece of false information."[12]

JOSHUA LAWRENCE CHAMBERLAIN

The exertions of the Gettysburg Campaign and battle left Chamberlain, who had suffered from "malarial fever" since the spring, exhausted. In early August 1863 he was granted sick leave to return home to Brunswick, Maine to rest and recuperate. But in mid-August Colonel James Rice, who assumed command of the 3rd Brigade, 2nd Division, 5th Corps after the death of Colonel Strong Vincent, was promoted to brigadier general. Brigadier General Charles Griffen, the division commander, wanted Chamberlain to assume command of the brigade. Chamberlain returned to the army although he had not fully recovered from his illness.

Charles Griffen was a hard-bitten regular army officer, but he recognized Chamberlain's ability as a soldier and recommended him for promotion to brigadier general. The recommendation failed to win approval and Chamberlain remained a colonel. During the fall campaign Chamberlain again fell ill and left the field. He returned at the commencement of Grant's Overland Campaign in command of the 20th Maine.

On June 5, after a month of battles with ghastly casualties, 5th Corps commander Major General Gouvernor K. Warren reorganized his command. Chamberlain received command of a brigade of six Pennsylvania regiments. The increased responsibility did not carry a promotion; Chamberlain remained a colonel. On June 18 he led his brigade in an assault poorly planned and coordinated by his superiors. During the attack a bullet struck him below the right hip, went through his body and lodged near the surface at his left hip. Through sheer force of will, he managed to remain on his feet for a few moments by using his sword to lean upon, and attempted to encourage his men. Loss of blood soon caused Chamberlain to sink to the ground, where he lay with the battle raging about him for nearly an hour. A detachment of artillerymen finally retrieved him from the field.

At the division hospital Chamberlain's wound was examined and pronounced mortal. An earlier recommendation from General Warren for Chamberlain's promotion to brigadier general was at that moment sitting at

army headquarters. Learning of Chamberlain's mortal wound, General George G. Meade immediately endorsed it and gave it to General Grant. Grant had been given the authority at the opening of the spring campaign to promote officers in the field for special acts of gallantry. He used that authority on June 20, 1864, to promote Chamberlain to brigadier general. Miraculously, Chamberlain survived his wounds.

Chamberlain returned home to recover. During his convalescence he was offered his old position at Bowdoin College. Despite pressure from his family to accept, he declined the offer and on November 18, 1864, returned to the army even though he still could not mount a horse without assistance or walk any distance. His wound continued to cause him intense pain and in January he traveled to Philadelphia where he had surgery to relieve his suffering. He again returned to Maine to convalesce. His wound was serious enough that he had ample and honorable reasons to accept a medical discharge and assume a civilian position. His parents strongly encouraged him to do so. But Chamberlain chose to return to the army. A letter he wrote to his mother explaining why he had made this decision provided insight into his courageous and irrepressible spirit, and his deep faith. He wrote:

> I owe the Country three years service. It is a time when every man should stand by his guns. And I am not scared or hurt enough yet to be willing to face the rear, when other men are marching to the front.
>
> It is true my incomplete recovery from my wounds would make a more quiet life desirable, & when I think of my young & dependent

family the whole strength of that motive to make the most of my life comes over me.

But there is no promise of life in peace, & no decree of death in war. And I am so confident of the sincerity of my motives that I can trust my own life & the welfare of my family in the hands of providence.[13]

On March 29, 1865, at the Battle of Quaker Road, Chamberlain received a severe wound that passed through his bridle arm and struck him a blow below the heart, where it was deflected by a pocket mirror and some papers he carried. Despite the wound, Chamberlain rallied and inspired his men to victory. His actions were so conspicuous that General Warren saw that Chamberlain received a brevet promotion to major general for gallantry in action.

Despite his most recent wound, Chamberlain remained in the field and participated in the smashing Union victory over George Pickett at Five Forks on March 31, 1865. Following Lee's surrender to Grant at Appomattox Court House, Chamberlain was selected to command the surrender ceremonies when the Confederate infantry formally surrendered their arms. On April 12, 1865, Chamberlain had his men arrayed in formation to receive the vanquished Confederate soldiers. At the head of the Confederate column rode Major General John B. Gordon, the fiery commander of the 2nd Corps, who sat his horse with head bowed and eyes cast down. "The momentous meaning of this occasion impressed me deeply," wrote Chamberlain. "I resolved to mark it by some token of recognition, which could be no other than a salute of arms."[14]

When the head of Gordon's column arrived opposite Chamberlain's troops a bugle sang out, "and instantly our whole line from right to left, regiment by regiment in succession, gives the soldier's salutation, from the 'order arms' to the old 'carry'—the marching salute." Gordon instantly recognized the bugle call, wheeled his horse to face his command and gave the order for each successive brigade to pass the Federal soldiers with the same position of the manual. Chamberlain recalled: "On our part not a sound of trumpet more, nor roll of drum; not a cheer, nor word nor whisper of vain-glorying, nor motion of man standing again at the order, but an awed stillness rather, and breath-holding, as if it were the passing of the dead!" It was one of the great moments in American history and one of Chamberlain's most memorable deeds, honoring a valiant enemy who was now a fellow countryman.[15]

Following the war, Chamberlain returned home to Maine a bona fide war hero. In 1866 he was elected governor of Maine by the largest majority in the state's history. He served in that post for four successive terms. Following his fourth term in 1871, he took the position of president of Bowdoin College, which he held until 1883. He remained active in veterans' organizations and was frequently asked to speak about the war. Chamberlain's wounds continued to trouble him and in April 1883 he had surgery to ease his suffering. The prospect of a long and slow recovery caused him to resign his position at Bowdoin College, and he devoted his time to managing his many business interests.

In 1893, Congress voted Chamberlain the Medal of Honor for gallantry at Gettysburg on July 2, 1863. He accepted the position of surveyor of Portland, Maine in 1900. The position was not demanding, which allowed Chamberlain time to write. He produced several articles about his war experiences and a beautifully written book on the Appomattox Campaign, which was published after his death as *The Passing of the Armies*.

Chamberlain's health continued to decline as a result of his wounds. Finally in 1914 they became infected and he passed away on February 24, 1914.

JOHN BUFORD

For Buford and his cavalry division the fighting at Gettysburg was merely a punctuation mark in a long, exhausting campaign that began in early June and did not conclude until mid-July, when Lee withdrew back into Virginia. In the course of the campaign the division suffered 1,160 casualties. But the end of the campaign did not mean a period of rest for Buford and his command. They were kept busy patrolling and reconnoitering to maintain contact with

the Confederates. The constant strain and physical demands placed upon Buford took their toll. In early August, while operating near the old Brandy Station battlefield he became so disgusted with the lack of support provided by the Union 12th Corps infantry under Major General Henry Slocum that he lost his typical equanimity and fired off an emotional dispatch to the Cavalry Corps commander, Major General Alfred Pleasonton:

> I am disgusted and worn out with the system that seems to prevail. There is so much apathy, and so little disposition to fight and co-operate that I wish to be relieved from the Army of the Potomac. I do not wish to put myself and soldiers in front where I cannot get a support short of 12 miles. The ground I gain I would like to hold...I am willing to serve my country, but I do not wish to sacrifice the brave men under my command.[16]

Brigadier General John Gibbon, a friend of Buford's, claimed that labors of the Gettysburg Campaign had fallen particularly hard upon the cavalry, and that, "Buford, one of the most hard-working of commanders fell victim to this strain." Buford took a brief leave of absence after this incident to return home to Kentucky. When he returned to the army in September, he resumed the arduous work of constant patrolling and probing of the enemy's front. In late October 1863 he received orders reassigning him to command the cavalry of the Army of the Cumberland. But the constant exposure and years of hard campaigning caught up with him and he was stricken with typhoid fever in early November. He took a leave of absence, but his health steadily deteriorated. When it became apparent that Buford would not live, President Lincoln directed that he be promoted to major general. He died on December 16 after learning of his promotion.

Colonel Charles Wainwright, the Union 1st Corps chief of artillery, noted Buford's death in his journal on December 20, 1863. His entry was a fitting epitaph for Buford:

> The army and the country have met with a great loss by the death of General John Buford. He was decidedly the best cavalry general we had, and was acknowledged as such in the army, though being no friend to newspaper reporters, he was made no more of in their reports than [Major General John F.] Reynolds was. In many respects he resembled Reynolds, being rough in his exterior, never looking after his own comfort, untiring on the march and in the su-pervision of all the militia of his command, quiet and unassuming in his manners. As General Hunt said: "Reynolds and Buford are the greatest losses this army has suffered."[17]

WINFIELD SCOTT HANCOCK

The severity of Hancock's wound on July 3, 1863, kept him out of action for many months, but he returned in command of his beloved 2nd Corps for Grant's 1864 Overland Campaign. In two months of constant fighting the 2nd Corps lost nearly 20,000 men. By the fall of 1864 it was fought out and so was Hancock. There was talk of him replacing Meade in command of the Army of the Potomac, but Hancock's Gettysburg wound had never healed properly and the rigors of corps command, let alone army command, were beyond his physical endurance. He received reassignment to Washington, where he helped to organize a reserve corps, but his part in active operations had ended.

His post required him to oversee the hanging of Mary Surratt and the others implicated in the Lincoln Assassination, a duty he found highly distasteful. He saw more clearly than others that Mrs. Surratt had been wrongly implicated and hoped that she might be reprieved. "I have been in many a battle and have seen death, and mixed with it in disaster and victory," he said to Judge John W. Clampitt, Mary Surratt's defense counsel. "I have been in a living hell of fire, and shell and grapeshot, and, by God, I'd sooner be there ten thousand times over than to give the order this day for the execution of that poor woman. But I am a soldier, sworn to obey, and obey I must."[18]

In 1866 Congress passed a resolution honoring him for his distinguished service at Gettysburg. He received promotion to major general in the regular army and was assigned to command the Department of Missouri, where he confronted troubles with Native Americans in the region. A year later he was assigned to command the volatile Department of Louisiana and Texas. Hancock opposed the oppressive policies of the Radical Republicans who controlled Congress and sought to punish the South by imposing military law upon the civilian population. As he prepared to assume his new duties Hancock clearly stated the stand he would take: "I am expected to exercise extreme military authority over those people. I shall disappoint them. I have not been educated to overthrow the civilian authorities in time of peace. I intend to recognize the fact that the Civil War is at an end." When he arrived at his headquarters in New Orleans, Hancock published General Order No. 40 which declared that civilian courts had jurisdiction over all crimes and offenses not involving forcible resistance to federal authority, guaranteed freedom of speech and of the press, and restored the right of habeas corpus. The order created a sensation, which Hancock knew it would. But he had done what he believed was rightfully and legally due the people of the South as United States citizens. The radical elements of Congress were outraged and prevented the order from winning approval. Hancock came under intense criticism for his alleged sympathy with former Confederates. This he could stand, but he received no support from his superiors for decisions he knew were legal and right, and he submitted his resignation from command of the department.[19]

In 1880 Hancock received the Democratic nomination for President. He conducted a campaign of high moral principles, and lost in one of the closest elections in U. S. history. Out of nine million ballots cast, James Garfield, his Republican opponent, clinched a victory by a margin of 7,023 popular votes. Hancock's wife recalled that she woke him at 5 a.m. on the morning after the election to tell him he had lost. "That is all right. I can stand it," he replied and went back to sleep. Political supporters and friends did not take the narrow defeat as easily and loudly declared that Garfield had won by fraud. But Hancock would have none of it. He declared, "the campaign is over and the true Christian spirit is to forgive and forget."[20]

Hancock's last years were marked by tragedy. In 1875, his daughter Ada died of typhoid fever. Then in 1883, his chief of staff William Mitchell died. The two men had been together since 1861, and Hancock, "regarded him with as much affection as he bestowed on one of his family."[21] Mitchell's death was followed by the death of Russell Hancock, Hancock's son, in 1884. Hancock's personal burdens were further deepened by the alcoholism of his twin brother, Hilary, for whom he was forced to provide financial support.

Hancock died February 7, 1886, as a result of an infection brought on by the lancing of a boil on his neck. Henry Slocum, who commanded the Union

12th Corps at Gettysburg, offered a simple estimation of Hancock as a soldier. He wrote: "On the field of battle he had no superior in either army."[22]

GEORGE GORDON MEADE

Meade, the commander of the Army of the Potomac and victor of Gettysburg, is allotted a mere cameo appearance in Shaara's novel. Shaara merely reflects the popular opinion of Meade as a grumpy, cautious, and barely competent general who won the battle because Lee lost it, not because of his own generalship. Edwin Coddington challenged this estimate of Meade in his classic study *The Gettysburg Campaign*. He found that while Meade may not have been brilliant, he had been highly competent and had made a major contribution to the Union victory.

Following Lee's retreat from the battlefield, Meade commenced a cautious pursuit for which he was sharply criticized. But his critics treated the 23,000 casualties his army had suffered in three days as a trifling inconvenience, and the loss of his two most trusted corps commanders, Hancock and Reynolds, as a matter of little consequence. Meade himself was exhausted. He wrote his wife on July 8:

> From the time I took command until today, now over ten days, I have not changed my clothes, have not had a regular nights rest & many nights not a wink of sleep and for several days did not even

wash my face & hand—no regular food and all the time in a state of mental anxiety. Indeed, I think I have lived as much in this time as in the last 30 years.[23]

Meade caught up with Lee on the banks of the Potomac River near Williamsport, Maryland, on July 12. The river was in flood and Lee had his back to it. The destruction of the Confederate army seemed inevitable. Yet Lee's position was highly formidable. His flanks were anchored upon the Potomac and earthworks sheltered his infantry and artillery. That night Meade called a council of his generals. He explained that he favored an all-out assault upon the enemy works on the 13th, but he put the question to a vote. Only two generals voted to attack. The rest wished to reconnoiter what was obviously a very strong position before mounting an attack. No one believed Lee could escape. But, unseen by Union scouts, Lee's engineers managed to lay a pontoon bridge over the Potomac and during the night, covered by a heavy rain, Lee crossed his army to Virginia.

The escape of Lee drew an immediate and angry reaction from Washington. Lincoln was greatly upset at the news and wrote a stinging letter of reproach to Meade, which he thought better of and did not send. But Union army chief of staff Henry W. Halleck sent a telegram that told Meade point-blank that the President was unhappy that the enemy had escaped, and that the army should begin an immediate pursuit. By the time he received Halleck's telegram, Meade had an opportunity to inspect the Confederate position. What he and his generals discovered was a most formidable position, which some compared in strength to the one Lee had occupied at Fredericksburg. Even General Oliver O. Howard, who had voted with Meade to attack, had his doubts that an attack on the 13th would have been successful after examining the Confederate works. With the realization that his men might have been slaughtered had he attacked, Halleck's telegram, sent from a perspective far removed from the actual circumstances at the front, infuriated Meade. He wired back: "Having performed my duty conscientiously and to be the best of my ability, the censure of the President conveyed in your dispatch...is in my judgment so undeserved that I feel compelled most respectfully to ask to be immediately relieved from the command of the army." Halleck responded with a dispatch of more gentle tone to sooth Meade's offended pride, but Meade grumbled in a letter to his wife that he did not believe he possessed the temperament to deal with the authorities in Washington.[24]

His temperament, never one of his strengths, did not improve with the pressures of army command. He lost his temper easily and his tongue lashings were greatly feared by staff and subordinates. One man described him "like a firework, always going bang at someone, and nobody ever knows who is going to catch it next, but all stand in a semi-terrified state."[25]

The pressure upon Meade to bring Lee's army to battle remained intense as summer gave way to fall. In September 1863, following the Union defeat at Chickamauga, the 11th and 12th Army Corps were transferred west, leaving Meade an army of only about 60,000 effectives. But Lee also had been weakened by the transfer of Longstreet's Corps. Nevertheless, Meade remained wary of risking his army in full-scale battle with Lee, unless it could be on his own terms. Lee did not intend to oblige Meade, and neither did he intend to fight with his depleted army unless he possessed a decided advantage. The result was a fall campaign of maneuvering punctuated by several small engagements, but no general battle. Meade suffered under difficult logistical problems and a lack of competent corps commanders, and Lee outmaneuvered him at nearly every turn. Meade admitted to his wife that it "was a deep game, and I am free to admit that in the playing of it he [Lee] has got the advantage of me."[26]

Although the fall campaign had not ended in success, neither could it be labeled a flat failure. Meade had accomplished something that no other commander of the Army of the Potomac had achieved. He refused to fight a battle simply because the authorities in Washington expected one. At the climactic moment of the Mine Run Campaign, Meade had brought his army up against Lee, who had entrenched behind Mine Run. An all-out assault was planned for November 30. However, early that morning General Gouvernor K. Warren discovered the Confederates had extended their trenches and improved their defenses to the point that the planned attack had no hope of success. Warren appealed to Meade that any attack would be a useless sacrifice of men. Meade agreed and canceled the assault. One Union veteran wrote that "the army, perhaps the Union cause was saved due to the clear judgement and military skill of those ground officers, Meade and Warren."[27]

Meade fully expected the failure of the Mine Run Campaign to lead to his relief from command of the army. It did not, but it provided fuel to Meade's enemies, most notably former 3rd Corps commander, Major General Daniel Sickles, who was seeking to discredit him in order to bring about his removal. But Meade weathered the storm of controversy, and in March 1864 he still commanded the Army of the Potomac when Ulysses S. Grant came east to assume command of all Union forces. When Grant informed Meade that he would attach his headquarters in the field with the Army of the Potomac, Meade offered to resign. It was not a professional pique that caused Meade to extend this offer. He thought Grant might want to place someone of his own choosing in the position. Grant recalled: "He urged that the work before us was of such vast importance to the whole nation that the feeling or the wishes of no one person should stand in the way of selecting the right men for all positions." Meade's forthright manner impressed Grant, who wrote: "This incident gave me an even more favorable opinion of Meade than did his great victory at

Gettysburg the July before. It is men who wait to be selected, and not those who seek, from whom we may always expect the most efficient service."[28]

Although Meade was caught in an embarrassing position, with Grant's headquarters attached to the Army of the Potomac, the arrangement worked better than expected. In general, Grant planned and Meade saw that his army carried out the details. The campaign that ensued was the bloodiest ever endured by an American army to that point. Always in the giant shadow of Grant, Meade nevertheless performed capably throughout the terrible spring campaign. But an incident that occurred in June 1864 guaranteed Meade's status as a behind-the-scenes player. A Philadelphia *Inquirer* reporter printed a story on June 2 that claimed Meade wanted to retreat back across the Rapidan on May 6, after a day of near disaster in the Wilderness. When Meade heard the reporter who had written the article had rejoined the army he called him to headquarters and without mincing words denounced him as a liar. He had the man mounted backwards on a mule wearing a sign that read "Libeler of the Press," and drummed him out of the army. The backlash of this event was an agreement among the army correspondents to shun Meade and give him credit for nothing. His name would not be mentioned in any reports from the army unless there was something negative to say about him. This would haunt Meade for the rest of his days and affect his place in history. To this day a common mistaken belief held by those with a casual interest in the American Civil War, is that Meade was relieved when Grant took command of all Union armies.[29]

While the press black-balled Meade, he continued to perform his duty in the most arduous, costly campaigning of the American Civil War. The fighting moved across northern Virginia to Petersburg and Richmond where it stalemated into trench warfare. Theodore Lyman, a volunteer aide at army headquarters, wrote in his journal of Meade: "I undertake to say that his handling of the troops...has been a wonder, without exaggeration, a wonder...I don't say that he is Napoleon, Caesar, and Alexander in one, only that he can handle 100,000 men and do it easy—a rare gift!"[30] It was Meade's fate, at the closing stages of the war, to do his duty faithfully and effectively, yet to have his successes upstaged by the dramatics of Major General Philip Sheridan, who won the glory of bringing Lee's army to bay at Appomattox Court House. Meade, who had done so much to bring about Lee's defeat, was not even present during the surrender ceremony on April 9.

Following the end of the war, Meade saw duty in several different military departments and districts. His most challenging work came in command of the third military district of the Department of the South, which included the states of Georgia, Florida, and Alabama. Meade commanded this district with characteristic fairness and integrity, earning the respect of its former Confederate citizens. When he left this assignment, the rector and wardens of St. Philip's

Church in Atlanta wrote him: "We shall ever remember you as an honest, unselfish and liberal Christian gentleman." No soldier who commanded during the Reconstruction years in the South could have asked for a greater compliment.[31]

With Grant's election as president in 1868, the positions of general of the army and lieutenant general in the regular army became available. Sherman, as expected, received the position of general of the army. Meade hoped he would be named lieutenant general. Grant gave the post to Sheridan. Bitterly disappointed, Meade wrote his wife: "you can imagine the force of this blow, but it is useless to repine over what cannot be remedied."[32]

Meade was assigned to duty in Philadelphia. His health, as a result of a serious wound he had received at the Battle of Glendale in July 1862, was poor. Nevertheless, he attended the dedication of the Soldiers' National Monument in Gettysburg in July, 1869, where he gave an eloquent and memorable speech. With typical courage, and disdain for popular political feelings, he called for the reburial of the Confederate dead in the National Cemetery. He said that although the Confederates were misguided in the cause they fought for, they were now countrymen again and deserving of an honorable burial. Meade's suggestion was never acted upon.

Pneumonia, brought on by his old Glendale wound, took Meade's life on November 6, 1872, while the country was celebrating Grant's second election to the presidency. He was fifty-six years old. Perhaps the most fitting epitaph to Meade, and to his unflinching character, was a sentence written by former aide Theodore Lyman to Meade's widow. It said, "We have lost a man who did not know what it was to be false."[33]

SUGGESTED READING
ON GETTYSBURG

The natural question for readers of *The Killer Angels* is, where do I go from here? What else is there to read on the Battle of Gettysburg? The answer is, more than you can imagine. There is more written on this particular battle than on any other military conflict in world history. A comprehensive, selectively annotated bibliography on the Gettysburg campaign by Richard Sauers, titled *The Gettysburg Campaign; A Bibliography*, (Greenwood Press, 1982), contains 2,757 entries. There are so many choices that deciding what to read is bewildering for the uninitiated. And there is a great quantity of writing on Gettysburg that is patently bad and should be left alone. The following bibliography surveys a fair sampling of good historical works on Gettysburg that the reader of *The Killer Angels* can select from to begin exploring the fascinating story of the battle and its aftermath.

GENERAL HISTORIES

Buel, Clarence and Robert Underwood, eds. *Battles and Leaders of the Civil War*. 4 vols. Castle, NJ: Century Company, 1884-1887. Some of the key participants of the battle, such as Longstreet and E. P. Alexander, wrote personal accounts of the battle for *Century Magazine*, which were later published in book form. Volume 3 covers the Gettysburg Campaign. This set has been reprinted numerous times and is easily obtainable at libraries and bookstores.

Catton, Bruce. *The Battle of Gettysburg*. New York: American Heritage Pub. Co., 1963. An easy read by one of the most gifted writers of Civil War history.

___. *Gettysburg: The Final Fury*. New York: Doubleday & Co., 1974. Catton's second work on Gettysburg. Aimed at a younger audience.

Clark, Champ. *Gettysburg: The Confederate High Tide*. Alexandria, VA: Time-Life Books, 1985. Part of the Time-Life multi-volume series The Civil War. Profusely illustrated, excellent maps, and a highly readable text.

Pfanz, Harry. *The Battle of Gettysburg*. Conshohocken, PA: Eastern National Park and Monument Association, 1994. A brief, but excellent 59 page book by a former National Park Service chief historian that serves as a fine introduction to the campaign and battle.

ADVANCED HISTORIES

Coddington, Edwin. *The Gettysburg Campaign: A Study in Command.* Reprint. Dayton, OH: Morningside Bookshop, 1979. Far and away the best campaign and battle study available. The research is exhaustive, and Coddington offers the most balanced assessment of the generalship of both armies available. However, it is not a book for the casual reader, with 574 pages of text and over 200 pages of endnotes. Although it is not a quick read, for anyone who wants to understand the campaign and battle it is time well spent.

Comte De Paris. *The Battle of Gettysburg.* Reprint. Baltimore: Butternut and Blue, 1987. Originally published in 1907. The Comte De Paris was a French nobleman who served as a volunteer aide with the Army of the Potomac in 1862, and in the post-Civil War period won a reputation as a historian of some repute. Although Paris did not have the wealth of source material that Coddington used, he interviewed, spoke to, and corresponded with a number of key officers who participated in the battle.

Tucker, Glen. *High Tide at Gettysburg.* Reprint. Dayton, OH: Morningside Bookshop, 1973. A well written, fast paced narrative, although the author's sympathies are clearly with the Confederate army. However, Tucker offers a fair and impartial assessment of Longstreet's performance at Gettysburg.

THE FIRST DAY

Gallagher, Gary, ed. *The First Day at Gettysburg.* Kent, OH: Kent State Univ. Press, 1992. An outstanding collection of four essays by leading historians on aspects of Union and Confederate leadership.

Hassler, Warren. *Crisis at the Crossroads.* Reprint. Gettysburg, PA: Stan Clark Books, 1986. The first and, for a time, the only modern study of this day of battle. Although readable it is dated and did not make use of unpublished sources.

Martin, David. *Gettysburg July 1.* Conshohocken, PA: Combined Books, 1995. A massive study of the first day of battle.

Shue, Richard. *Morning at Willoughby Run.* Gettysburg, PA: Thomas Publications, 1995. Examines the morning fighting on July 1 in detail.

THE SECOND DAY

Desjardin, Thomas A. *Stand Firm Ye Boys From Maine.* Gettysburg, PA: Thomas Publications, 1995. An outstanding study of the 20th Maine at Gettysburg. Provides a balanced account of their accomplishments on Little Round Top.

Gallagher, Gary, ed. *The Second Day at Gettysburg*. Kent, OH: Kent State Univ. Press, 1993. Essays on leadership and command on July 2, 1863.

Norton, Oliver. *The Attack and Defense of Little Round Top*. Reprint. Dayton, OH: Morningside Bookshop, 1991. Norton served at Gettysburg as Colonel Strong Vincent's orderly. His book contains a series of papers, essays, articles, letters, and official reports written by Union and Confederate participants who figured in the struggle for Little Round Top.

Pfanz, Harry. *Gettysburg: The Second Day*. Chapel Hill, NC: Univ. of North Carolina Press, 1987. A massive, yet highly readable study of the second day's fighting on the Union left and center.

———. *Culp's Hill and Cemetery Hill*. Chapel Hill, NC: Univ. of North Carolina Press, 1994. Dr. Pfanz's sequel to *Gettysburg: The Second Day*, examines the struggle for the two key hills on the Union right from July 1-3. Superbly researched and well written.

Pullen, John. *The Twentieth Maine*. Reprint. Dayton, OH: Morningside Bookshop, 1994. A fine history of this famous regiment during the war.

THE THIRD DAY

Gallagher, Gary, ed. *The Third Day at Gettysburg and Beyond*. Chapel Hill, NC: Univ. of North Carolina Press, 1994. The third in Dr. Gallagher's excellent series.

Harrison, Kathleen Georg, and John W. Busey. *Nothing But Glory*. Gettysburg, PA: Thomas Publications, 1994. A richly detailed account of Pickett's Division and their famous assault upon Cemetery Ridge on July 3. Also includes a complete roster of every soldier in Pickett's Division present at Gettysburg.

Stewart, George. *Pickett's Charge: A Microhistory*. Dayton, OH: Morningside Bookshop, 1980. Wonderfully readable and highly detailed account of Pickett's Charge from both the Union and Confederate perspective.

SPECIALIZED WORKS

Gettysburg was such a huge event that books on the campaign and battle tell only part of the story. Numerous other works depart from the study of tactics, strategy, and command to explore other areas.

Coco, Gregory. *A Vast Sea of Misery*. Gettysburg, PA: Thomas Publications, 1988. A thorough description of the hospitals that treated nearly 27,000 wounded.

———. *A Strange and Blighted Land, Gettysburg: The Aftermath of the Battle*. Gettysburg, PA: Thomas Publications, 1995. Using a wealth of source material the author tells the often ignored story of what happened after the battle ended and the armies departed.

Conklin, Eileen. *Women of Gettysburg*. Gettysburg, PA: Thomas Publications, 1994. Hundreds of woman helped tend the wounded and perform other important chores during and after the battle. This is their story.

Frassanito, William. *Gettysburg: A Journey in Time*. New York: Charles Scribner's Sons, 1975. An outstanding, and sometimes haunting, study of the photographers and the photographs they took immediately after the battle. Frassanito hunted out nearly every location that the original photographs were taken on the battlefield and provides a modern view to compare to the historic one.

——. *Early Photography at Gettysburg*. Gettysburg, PA: Thomas Publications, 1995. An exhaustive work, rich in detail, and fascinating to read. Includes wartime or early postwar photographs not included in *Gettysburg: A Journey in Time*.

Wills, Gary. *Lincoln at Gettysburg*. New York: Simon and Schuster, 1992. A Pulitzer Prize winning book on Lincoln and the Gettysburg Address.

Major Characters

Nearly every major character of *The Killer Angels* is the subject of a book-length biography, except for Lewis Armistead. Some wrote books themselves, such as Chamberlain and Longstreet.

Chamberlain, Joshua L. *The Passing of the Armies*. Reprint. Dayton, OH: Morningside Bookshop, 1985. Chamberlain's story of the Appomattox Campaign, published after his death. One of the most beautifully written books to emerge from the war.

Cleaves, Freeman. *Meade of Gettysburg*. Norman, OK: Univ. of Oklahoma Press, 1991. A solid biography of the general who won the Battle of Gettysburg.

Freeman, Douglas S. *R. E. Lee*. 4 vols. Reprint. New York: Macmillan, 1991. Unquestionably, the best biography of Lee, despite Freeman's adoration for his subject.

——. *Lee's Lieutenants*. 3 vols. New York: Charles Scribner's Sons, 1944. This majestic study covers the brigade, division, and corps leadership of the Army of Northern Virginia.

Jordan, David. *Winfield Scott Hancock*. Bloomington, IN: Indiana Univ. Press, 1988. A scholarly study of Hancock that covers his post-Civil War years very well.

Longacre, Edward. *General John Buford: A Military Biography*. Conshohocken, PA: Combined Books, 1995. The only book-length biography of Buford presently available. Adequate, but not the definitive biography.

Longstreet, James. *From Manassas to Appomattox.* Reprint. New York: DeCapo Press, 1992. Longstreet's own, and often biased, story of his wartime experiences.

Motts, Wayne. *Trust in God and Fear Nothing.* Gettysburg, PA: Farnsworth House Military Impressions, 1994. A brief booklet on Lewis B. Armistead by the leading authority on his life.

Nolan, Alan. *Lee Reconsidered.* Chapel Hill, NC: Univ. of North Carolina Press, 1991. Nolan offers a fresh perspective on Lee that challenges some accepted opinions on his strategic and tactical thinking.

Phipps, Michael and John Peterson. *The Devil's to Pay: John Buford, USA.* Gettysburg, PA: Farnsworth House Military Impressions, 1995. A well researched, concise biography of Buford.

Piston, William Garrett. *Lee's Tarnished Lieutenant: James Longstreet and His Place in Southern History.* Athens, GA: Univ. of Georgia Press, 1990. Piston does a particularly fine job on Longstreet's postwar life, and on how the tarnished and controversial image of him emerged.

Trulock, Alice Rains. *In The Hands of Providence: Joshua L. Chamberlain and the American Civil War.* Chapel Hill, NC: Univ. of North Carolina Press, 1992. The most recent biography of Joshua L. Chamberlain. Thoroughly researched but uncritical in content.

Tucker, Glen. *Hancock the Superb.* New York: Bobbs-Merrill, 1960. The earliest of two modern biographies of Hancock. Well written but does not cover Hancock's postwar career as thoroughly as David Jordan.

Wert, Jeffry. *James Longstreet: The Confederacy's Most Controversial Soldier.* New York: Simon and Schuster, 1994. Extensively researched and well written. The most recent biography of Longstreet.

Gettysburg is also the topic of a fine bi-annual magazine, titled appropriately, *The Gettysburg Magazine*, published by Morningside Bookshop in Dayton, Ohio.

The above books, and those cited in the notes, represent but a fraction of what is available for those readers of *The Killer Angels* who wish to move beyond the pages of a novel into the history of what really happened. Those who do will find that the actual events and people who participated in them are more exciting than fiction.

> All around, strange, mingled roar—shouts of defiance, rally, and desperation; and underneath, murmured entreaty and stifled moans; gasping prayers, snatches of Sabbath song, whispers of loved names; everywhere men torn and broken, staggering, creeping, quivering on the earth, and dead faces with strangely fixed eyes staring stark into the sky. Things which cannot be told—nor dreamed.
>
> —Colonel Joshua L. Chamberlain, *Through Blood and Fire*

NOTES

THE NOVEL AS HISTORY

1. For a discussion of Lee's consideration of Longstreet's proposal for a strategic turning movement, see Edwin Coddington, *The Gettysburg Campaign: A Study in Command*, (New York: Charles Scribner's Sons, 1968), 361-362. Also see Sir Frederick Maurice, ed., *An Aide de Camp of Lee, Being the Papers of Colonel Charles Marshall*, (Boston: Little, Brown Co., 1927), 232. Marshall was Lee's personal secretary.
2. Theodore Lyman, *Meade's Headquarters*, (Boston: Atlantic Monthly Press, 1922), 21. Michael Phipps, *The Devil's to Pay: John Buford, USA*, (Gettysburg, PA: Farnsworth House Military Impressions, 1995), 30.
3. Michael Shaara, *The Killer Angels*, (New York: Random House, 1974), 42.
4. John H. Calef, "Gettysburg Notes; The Opening Gun," *Journal of the Military Service Institution of the United States*, (New York: Charles B. Richardson, 1907), 40-58.
5. Shaara, 39-41.
6. Shaara, 38.
7. War Department, *War of the Rebellion; A Compilation of the Official Records of the Union and Confederate Armies*, Vol. 27, pt. 1, 923. Hereafter referred to as *OR*. The *Official Records* contain the official battle reports and correspondence of all military operations conducted during the Civil War in 127 volumes. The Gettysburg Campaign is covered in Volume 27 parts 1-3.
8. Birkett Fry to John Bachelder, 2/10/1888, John B. Bachelder Papers, Copy at Gettysburg National Military Park Library. The Original Bachelder Papers are located at the New Hampshire Historical Society and represent the largest collection of first-hand accounts of the Battle of Gettysburg in existence. They have recently been transcribed and published by Morningside Bookshop of Dayton, Ohio in three volumes.
9. *OR* Vol. 27, Pt. 1, 185. Robert K. Beecham, *Gettysburg: The Pivotal Battle of the Civil War*, (Chicago: A. C. McClure, 1911), 69. Beecham served with the 2nd Wisconsin at Gettysburg.
10. Shaara, 140-149.
11. John B. Gordon, *Reminiscences of the Civil War*, (Reprint, Dayton, OH: Morningside Press, 1981), 154.
12. *OR* Vol. 27, Pt. 2, 555; Pt. 1, 366.
13. Gary Gallagher, *First Day at Gettysburg*, (Kent, OH: Kent State University Press, 1992), 56.

14. S. R. Johnston to Fitz Lee, 2/16/1878, S. R. Johnston MSS, Library of Congress; Typescript Copy GNMP Library File 4-11i1; Coddington, 373. S. R. Johnston to Fitz Lee, 2/16/1878, S. R. Johnston MSS, Library of Congress; Typescript Copy GNMP Library File 4-11i1; Coddington, 373.
15. Shaara, 189. When Lee reorganized the Army of Northern Virginia after the Battle of Chancellorsville, Longstreet had advocated McLaws' promotion to one of the new corps commands that were created. He did not do so for Pickett or Hood. See Robert K. Krick, "I Consider Him a Humbug," *Virginia County Civil War*, Volume V, (1986), 30. Lafayette McLaws, "Gettysburg," Southern Historical Society Papers, Vol. 7, 68. The Southern Historical Society Papers represent one of the greatest collections of articles ever published on the Confederate experience during the war.
16. Shaara, 189.
17. A. L. Long, *Memoirs of Robert E. Lee*, (New York: J. M. Stoddart, Co., 1886, 1887), 281-282.
18. John B. Hood, *Advance and Retreat*, (Reprint, New York: DeCapo Press, 1994), 57.
19. Coddington, 378; Shaara, 193.
20. Johnston to Fitz Lee, 2/11/1878, Johnston MSS; James Longstreet, *Manassas to Appomattox*, (Reprint, New York: DeCapo Press, 1992), 365-366; Johnston to Lafayette McLaws, 7/27/1892, Johnston MSS.
21. Lafayette McLaws, "The Battle of Gettysburg," Paper Read Before the Confederate Veterans Association, April 17, 1896, GNMP Library File 5-Lafayette McLaws.
22. McLaws letter was published in Robert K. Krick, "I Consider Him a Humbug," *Virginia Country's Civil War*, Volume 5 (1986).
23. Moxley Sorrel, *Recollections of a Confederate Staff Officer*, (Jackson, TN: McCowat-Mercer Press, 1958), 157-158.
24. Oliver Norton, *The Attack and Defense of Little Round Top*, (Reprint, Dayton, OH: Morningside Press, 1983), 264.
25. *Ibid.*, 130-132.
26. Ellis Spear Recollections, GNMP; Elisha Coan Memoirs, Elisha Coan Papers, Hawthorne-Longfellow Library, Brunswick, ME. A copy is in the GNMP Library.
27. Joshua Chamberlain, "Through Blood and Fire," *Gettysburg Magazine*, No. 6 (January, 1992), 55. Dedication of the Twentieth Maine Monuments at Gettysburg, (Waldboro, ME, 1891), Copy GNMP Library File 6-ME20; Spear recollections, GNMP Library, File 6-ME20.
28. Shaara, 312.
29. *OR*, Vol. 27, Pt. 2, 308.
30. *Ibid.*, 447.
31. Shaara, 299-300.
32. Gary Gallagher, ed., *Fighting for the Confederacy*, (Chapel Hill, NC: Univ. of North Carolina Press, 1989), 254.
33. *Ibid.*, 254-255; James Longstreet, "Lee in Pennsylvania," *The Annals of the War, Written by Leading Participants, North and South*, (Reprint, Dayton, OH: Morningside Press, 1988), 430.
34. Shaara, 339.

35. Arthur Freemantle, *Three Months in the Confederate States*, (Reprint, Ohama, NE: Univ. of Nebraska Press, 1991), 214-215.

THE PEOPLE

1. Douglas S. Freeman, *Lee's Lieutenants: A Study in Command*, (New York: Charles Scribner's Sons, 1971), Vol. 3, 357.
2. Horace Porter, "The Surrender at Appomattox Court House," in Clarence Buel and Robert Underwood, *Battles and Leaders of the Civil War*, Vol. 4, (Reprint, New York: Castle Books, 1956), 743.
3. Douglas S. Freeman, *R. E. Lee*, (New York: Charles Scribner's Sons, 1935), Volume 4, 196.
4. *Ibid.*, 428.
5. McLaws was exonerated of all charges levied against him by Longstreet. He did not serve again with the Army of Northern Virginia. To his credit, McLaws was not embittered by Longstreet's actions against him and the two maintained a cordial (not warm) relationship after the war.
6. William G. Piston, *Lee's Tarnished Lieutenant: James Longstreet and His Place in Southern History*. (Athens, GA: Univ. of Georgia Press, 1987), 86.
7. Edward P. Alexander to Frederic Bancroft, October 30, 1904, quoted in Donald B. Sanger and Thomas R. Hay, *James Longstreet*, (Baton Rouge: Louisiana State Univ. Press, 1952), 434.
8. William W. Wood, "Pickett's Charge at Gettysburg," *The Compiler*, 22 August 1877, quoted in Kathleen Georg Harrison and John W. Busey, *Nothing But Glory*, (Hightstown, NJ: Longstreet House, 1987), 194.
9. Charles B. Flood, *Lee: The Last Years*, (Boston: Houghton Mifflin, 1981), 230-232.
10. *OR*, Vol. 27, Pt. 2, 321.
11. Freeman, *Lee's Lieutenants*, Vol. 3, 426.
12. *Ibid.*, 432.
13. Chamberlain to his parents, quoted in Alice Trulock, *In The Hands of Providence*, (Chapel Hill, NC: Univ. of North Carolina Press, 1992), 225.
14. Joshua Chamberlain, *The Passing of the Armies*, (Reprint, Dayton, OH: Morningside Bookshop, 1985), 260.
15. *Ibid.*, 261.
16. *OR*, Vol. 27, Pt. 3, 835.
17. Allan Nevins, ed., *Diary of Battle: The Personal Journals of Colonel Charles S. Wainwright*, (Reprint, Gettysburg, PA: Stan Clark Books, 1995), 309.
18. Glen Tucker, *Hancock the Superb*, (Reprint, Dayton, OH: Morningside Bookshop, 1973), 272; "Winfield S. Hancock: A Personality Profile," *Civil War Times Illustrated*, August, 1968, 10.
19. Tucker, *Hancock the Superb*, 47.
20. Anne Hancock, *Reminiscences of Winfield Scott Hancock*, (New York: Charles L. Webster, 1887), 172; New York Herald, November 5, 1880, as quoted in Glen Tucker, *Hancock the Superb*, 304.
21. Tucker, 305.
22. Tucker, *Hancock the Superb*, 174.

23. George G. Meade, Jr., *Life and Letters of George Gordon Meade*, (New York: Charles Scribner's Sons, 1913), Vol. 2, 132-133.
24. *OR* 27, Pt. 1, 92-94.
25. Joseph P. Cullen, "George Gordon Meade," *Civil War Times Illustrated*, Volume XIV, May, 1975, 44.
26. Meade to his Wife, October 21, 1863, quoted in Meade Jr., *Life and Letters of George G. Meade*, 154.
27. Freeman Cleaves, *Meade of Gettysburg*, (Norman, OK: Univ. of Oklahoma Press, 1960), 212-213.
28. William S. and Mary Drake McFeely, *Personal Memoirs of U. S. Grant and Selected Letters 1839-1865*, (New York: Viking Press, 1990), 470.
29. There is a full explanation of the repercussions for Meade in Freeman Cleaves' biography of Meade, *Meade of Gettysburg*.
30. George Agassiz, *Meade's Headquarters, 1863-1865, Letters of Colonel Theodore Lyman from the Wilderness to Appomattox*, (Boston: 1922), 271-273. One of the finest collections of letters on the Civil War. Lyman was a magnificent observer and writer.
31. Cleaves, 346; Meade, Jr., *Life and Letters*, Vol. 2, 300; Cleaves, 351.
32. Meade, Jr., *Life and Letters*, Vol. 2, 300.
33. Cleaves, 351.